MEN

—OF—

COTTA

KIM ROSE

iUniverse, Inc.
Bloomington

Men of Cotta

iUniverse books may be ordered through booksellers or by contacting:

iUniverse
1663 Liberty Drive
Bloomington, IN 47403
www.iuniverse.com
1-800-Authors (1-800-288-4677)

ISBN: 978-1-4759-1927-1 (sc)
ISBN: 978-1-4759-1928-8 (e)

Printed in the United States of America

iUniverse rev. date: 5/26/2012

My sincere thanks to the people at iUniverse,
who have been gracious, knowledgeable, and
helpful in getting this book published.

Thanks also to Jewels for the editing… and to
Jared for the assistance with grammar.

You can't blame a writer
for what the characters say.

– Truman Capote

for us…

1. AUNTIE STEPHANIE

It was that inevitable passage, that discouraging time of transition, common enough I suppose yet difficult nonetheless. My dear, sweet, precious, loving, aging Aunt Stephanie was becoming more than we could handle. She was Mom's only sibling. I felt especially close to her, I guess in part because she was much younger than Mom, and my first recollections of her were as the energetic teenager who babysat me. She would read to me and cuddle me to sleep. It was hard to believe she was already moving into some kind of dementia. We had tests run on her, with inconclusive results.

I thought her much too young for senility, she hardly seemed older than I, only a little more than ten years my senior. But a doctor assured us that retention loss could begin even in 40-somethings. She'd never married, had no children that we knew of, was all alone.

I could relate. My father had passed on from cancer when I was young, and Mom never remarried. I was an only child. Ever since Mom had died four years ago, caring for "Auntie S" (as my wife Deirdre and I affectionately called her) had stretched my family's patience to the limit. We needed to find a "home" for her. What with the slow departure of her memory, I'm not sure she entirely understood what we were trying to explain to her. She busied herself with her potted plants, which were mostly dying, and her mixed-media water color and crayon art, which

1

was becoming increasingly incoherent – projects that reflected her disintegrating lot in life. Old age is a cruel mistress.

Steph had started misplacing things. We'd find half-eaten sandwiches in the washing machine, her dirty clothes in the fridge. More troubling, she had a propensity for wandering off, and on ever more frequent occasions gave Deirdre and me scare upon scare as we searched the neighborhood in vain for a sign of her trail – a dropped lilac hanky, a day-glo pot holder, her big fuchsia shoulder bag, an orthopedic flip-flop, peanut shells, anything. She would more often than not find her way to the nearby casino where she bummed smokes, weaseled drinks, watched the flashing lights on the machines, and generally socialized.

I could handle the complaints from casino management, but it was no way to live.

Deirdre wanted to have a tracking device implanted in her, but that struck me as cold and harsh, uncaring.

So it was that I went delving into the nefarious world of the "assisted living community." The idea of warehousing my own flesh and blood in one of those institutions was discomforting to say the least. The potential cost of such a placement was riveting enough, what with Stephanie's minimal medical support plan, but it was the general reputation for uncleanliness and uncaring throughout these facilities that troubled me most.

One of my colleagues at the firm offered some advice which turned out to be helpful. He said his family had discovered one could find better deals and more sympathetic service in smaller towns. I set a two-hundred mile radius and searched the area on my iSomething. I paid virtual visits to several facilities before finally driving to the Peaceful Pastures Assisted Living Complex in Burgfort, Iowa and deciding on it. I was struck by its motto, "Whatever Works," which implied a possible, welcome flexibility. And it was a large institution, several hundred were living there, which I thought might afford much activity and interaction. Then again, all such places seemed to be full of seniors these days. People were living so long.

Auntie Stephanie had not been consulted before the big decision was made; we felt it would unduly upset her. We hoped her Alzheimer's would perhaps carry us through the delicate relocation from the basement suite in our house to the much-nicer double quarters she would share with her new roommate at the retirement home. It was my brother-in-law Dallas who came up with the idea of telling her we were taking her to a hotel while we went on an extended European vacation.

As the fateful weekend approached, I packed her belongings and clothing with doting care. On several occasions, Deirdre would find me in tears, holding some little keepsake or faded photograph I'd stumbled upon, one that had a richly sentimental history. My poor, blessed Auntie S had been such a beautiful child, pretty and laughing, blonde curls. There were pictures from her wild youth. She had filled out splendidly – short, buxom, and cute. When her parents had refused to let her go to that big rock festival in New England in the 1960s, *Roadstock* or *WolfTrap* or however you called it, she ran away from home, at age 13 no less, took off with some older guys in a Volkswagen van. Mom said she hadn't done drugs there, but she had done a lot of men. My grandparents had been furious with her, but even back then she was uncontrollable, a natural rebel.

She had been a serviceable college student, until she dropped out and went west. Mom never talked about it. Steph had also been a hippie of the first magnitude. In a family of taciturn blue-bloods, this had not been well-received.

As far as I was concerned though, my goodness, the Sixties had been 60 or 70 years ago and bygones were bygones. I loved her, pure and simple.

Steph's youthful vitality showed no signs of waning. But there was the wear and tear on her vitals and that vanishing memory and, sigh, it made me consider my own mortality. Our two kids were already grown, off to school and beyond.

It had all come to pass way too soon, and there I was, filling my van and Deirdre's car with boxes on a sizzling July Saturday morning. Then we loaded up Auntie S, programmed the destination into the vehicles, and set out in caravan for Burgfort, a little over two hours away across the state line. Steph rode with me in the van's front lounge area, busying herself by carefully and laboriously cutting paper dolls out of an AARP magazine. She had always refused to wear a seat belt, so there was this intermittent mumbling from the console the entire trip, but because I felt it might be the last time she and I were ever driving anywhere together, at least with her alive, I let it go.

The Peaceful Pastures nursing home, and Burgfort itself for that matter, were exactly as I had left them when I'd initialed the agreements on Stephanie's behalf a month prior. I got the impression that change was not a driving force in that lazy hamlet. The town appeared to be some kind of anachronism, suspended if not halted in yesteryear.

The Complex itself was a sprawling, two-story red brick affair without frills. It had grown haphazardly, with new additions tacked on as needed, a small town in and of itself. Fortunately, the signage was first-rate, and it didn't take us long to find the loading dock. Several staff members warmly greeted us there and helped empty our vehicles.

We had warned the administration about Auntie Stephanie's penchant for wandering off, and a pleasant, officious nurse took charge of her immediately, hustling her away for tests. This was comforting. Deirdre and I set to unpacking, and in no time we had Auntie's spacious room all cozy, her bureau drawers filled with clothing, her closet carefully organized, her most precious mementos on a quaint little corner hutch, her art supplies basket and easel by the easy chair. In spite of her disintegrating cognition, she had insisted on taking her massive power vibrator, which she called *Steely Dan* for some reason. Try as we might we could not dissuade her on that disquieting issue. After some discussion, we decided to leave it on her nightstand. Deirdre refused to touch it.

We hung Steph's treasured, framed photos on the walls, along with her flat-screen iEverything, which she called her *Magic Mirror*. Her toiletries were put in place in the medicine cabinet in her small, private bath.

Deirdre, who had developed an agenda which no longer included anyone but her, had to get back to the city for a business appointment, so she took off in the car, leaving me to help get Auntie S oriented. The staff suggested I head to the large community room in the front of the building while they finished the tests and helped her fill out a battery of legal forms which I would cyber sign on her behalf.

The parlor was billed as the hub of activities at Peaceful Pastures, furnished with a multitude of mismatched couches and easy chairs. End tables held reading materials of all kinds – books and publications, various devices like weathered Kindles and Nooks and iWhatchamahoozits. There were bookcases against the walls and an enormous 3D TV at the far end of the hall. On both sides of the room were impressive picture windows extending from floor to ceiling. Out the windows was Iowa countryside – rolling hills, a small meandering stream that ran through a pristine meadow, and huge shade trees dressed in summer greenery.

I was thinking it perfect, as I stood in the entrance and gazed across the room at the backs of little heads sticking up over stuffed sofas – gray and blue and pink hair everywhere. Not much movement, no hum of conversation. The occasional electric cart was parked to assist those for whom independent locomotion was no longer an option. It was a garden of fragile, wrinkled, inconsequential souls, alone with their thoughts, seemingly of no lingering use or endeavor, their labors finished, diminishing lights dimming, spinning quietly off into the ether against an underlying background hum of medical and technological gimcrackery and a slight, pervasive smell of tapioca.

My eyes panned slowly from one side of the room to the other, my gaze initially passing the two of them for an instant, then stopping in space and immediately returning to a decrepit couple sitting on a couch facing me. The woman was unremarkable, a neatly dressed, prim, plump remnant of femininity in baggy jeans and a black T-shirt which said "Lucky You" in hot red lettering across an ample, albeit drooping, bosom. The man was a bit larger than the general male population, bald as a cue ball, with a three-day growth of white whiskers. What attracted my attention was not so much the twosome's appearance, but their unique way of interrelating. They sat side-by-side, motionless, each with a hand in the other's lap.

It was so unfitting, so unseemly, I was instantly alarmed. As I stared at the man's face, his eyes closed, a slight smile on his lips, and followed his arm down to where his hand nestled between the woman's bulky thighs, I was suddenly alerted to the grim reality of Auntie Stephanie, whose sexual past was florid to say the least, in the same building with such a wanton predator.

I stood for a bit, flummoxed, wondering what to do. My first impulse was to walk over and confront him, but unfamiliar as I was with the prevailing folkways of the establishment, I opted for caution over valor. Still, weren't there rules? Then again, what exactly did one do with an elderly lothario? What sort of punishment could be inflicted or exacted? As I was mulling that over, I noticed a custodial tech on the far side of room managing a floor bot that was cleaning carpets and washing baseboards. I headed over towards him, giving me an excuse to pass by the very couch upon which the old bald man was ensconced, so I might briefly observe him up close, get a feel for the situation.

As I strode by him, I felt a surprisingly powerful, off-putting aura and was glad to move on to the bot guy. "Pardon me," I said, my voice lowered, "but that man behind me, with the woman next to him on the couch, who is he?"

The tech looked over my shoulder. "Rotzinger," he replied with a shake of his head.

"Rotzinger?" I repeated.

"Yeah."

"Know anything about him?"

"Not much. Been here a few years. Kind of a pain in the ass."

"Can something be done?" I tentatively offered.

"About what?"

"That guy, Rotzinger."

"I dunno, whattaya want done?"

He had me there. I tried to think of what exactly the problem was, other than a general sense of abhorrent tastelessness. The woman was obviously an adult. The behavior could not quite be considered lewd or lascivious; it didn't rise to that level. It was simply disgusting.

The man chuckled. "Can't throw him out, they need the money.

Maybe confine him to his room? I'm not sure anybody gives a damn anymore anyway."

"Well," I asked, "where's he from?"

He had now redirected his gaze to the bot. "Around here somewhere, I think, a local."

"Any kin?"

He looked at me. "Listen," he said, "most folks here, they don't get no visitors. It's like they been forgot. Kinda sad. I heard maybe he gotta daughter. If he do, she don't come 'round."

"That it?"

The tech scratched his chin absent-mindedly and glanced down to where the bot was scrubbing. "I tell ya man, clients here, a lot of 'em don't remember much. Kind of a blessing I guess. When he does talk, ain't about his family. I'm not sure he even remembers them." He shook his head and patted a wall for emphasis

"Too bad," I muttered, not wanting to appear unfeeling.

"Yeah, most folks here, they obsess on something, keep going back to that same thing."

"Oh really," I said. "That makes sense, come to think of it. My grandma, when she was old, kept going back to some house she'd lived in when her kids were born, had a big garden in back. She adored that garden."

The man furrowed his brow for a moment, then his eyes opened wide and his face brightened. "Ya know, Rotzinger keeps goin' on about a house too."

So he was housebroken. He had lived in one at some point.

The bot ran over one of my shoes, leaving a trail of suds. The custodian didn't notice it. "Cotta House," he continued. "Rotz has an old shirt, says *Cotta* on it. Don't know what that means." His attention returned to the bot.

Somewhat reassured, I walked back across the communal area and ambled down a couple of hallways until I found Auntie Stephanie's room. She seemed in terrific spirits as she sat and bounced on her new bed. The nurse told me everything was set, then bustled out to another vista. There was no sign of any roommate. "I like this hotel," Auntie S announced, "it's got all my stuff in it."

Then she waved, shot out the door, and disappeared down the hall.

I was suddenly all by myself. Auntie Steph was gone. It hit me, how much I'd miss her. Had I done the right thing? I felt empty as I stared at her belongings. I already missed her. My heart ached.

I walked slowly with resignation back to the front desk to finish up the cyberwork, and as I got in my van, I silently vowed to visit her often.

I dozed fitfully while it drove me back to the city.

2. ROTZINGER

The next Saturday saw me motoring through what meteorologists said was becoming the hottest July on record for the ninth year running, to check up on sweet Auntie Stephanie at the Assisted Living Complex. Deirdre was busy "tidying up in Auntie S's wake" as she indelicately put it, so I was alone with my thoughts in the air-conditioned comfort of my electric vehicle. The highway wound through rolling hills and forests, the trip puter guiding me effortlessly to Burgfort.

I asked the van to take me down Main Street so I could look at the shops. I was hoping to get some flowers for Stephanie, but there wasn't much to be had in the way of commerce. Most of the stores had gone out of business, the buildings old and in a moribund state of disrepair. The town wasn't much of a going concern. There were a couple of gas/hydro/electro stations, some grain elevators, a few taverns. That was it.

The front-desk staff at Peaceful Pastures welcomed me cheerfully, directing me to my aunt's room. She wasn't there. When I went back to the lobby, the ladies on duty told me with great enthusiasm that Stephanie had instantly become a social butterfly and was constantly fluttering about. They assured me she loved the place and was in good shape and good spirits.

I went immediately to the communal area, fearing Steph had already fallen into the clutches of Rotzinger, but upon a cursory reconnoiter of the room was put at ease by her absence. Rotzinger was there, however, sitting in the same spot, next to the same plump lady, his eyes closed. On her periwinkle T-shirt was emblazoned "Get-Down Granny" in bright yellow lettering. All around the room, old people were reading, sleeping, or simply staring off into space.

I decided to chat him up, since he didn't appear busy. I walked over to him, grabbed a nearby folding chair, and sat down. The lady was snoring, but Rotzinger opened his eyes slowly, as if he heard my approach, and looked at me. He said hi and extended his left hand.

I shook it gently, noting a slight, lingering power in it, and returned his greeting. "I'm Marvin," I said.

"Call me *Supreme*," he stated with some authority.

I wasn't sure I'd heard him right. "Beg pardon?"

"Actually, it's *Number One Supreme*. But just *Supreme* will do."

"Someone told me your name was Rotzinger."

"Well, it is. You can call me Rotz if you'd like. Or *Rotz Number One Supreme*. My friends call me *Supreme* though."

Was he toying with me? Was he serious? He seemed serious. He had friends?

I was tentative. "Well, OK then, nice to meet you, Mr. Supreme."

His head dropped with disappointment and a hint of frustration. It slowly shook back and forth. "No," he said softly, staring down, "just *Supreme*. No *Mister*."

We were off to a shaky start, I thought, but when I called him *Supreme* he seemed placated – he even brightened.

"Can we talk a bit?" I asked him.

"Sure," he replied. "Just a sec…" And he moved to get up with what almost passed for alacrity. When he stood, the old lady who was leaning against him collapsed onto the big sofa cushions where he'd been sitting. He ignored her and hobbled to the electric cart parked at the end of the couch. I noticed a long antenna on the hood of the thing. Attached to it was a little flesh-colored pennant with the word "Teutons" printed in purple block letters. It had a bumper sticker which read: *2 Nuts 2 Die*.

Once seated in it, he said with what struck me as a practiced command, "Take your chair and follow me," and drove over to an empty spot by a picture window. I did as told, placing the chair beside him and sitting on it. His face was pleasant. All the wrinkles gave him a certain gravitas. His eyes were bright and sharp.

"Lovely view," I said, tentatively.

"Gets old," he said, "like everything else around here." He slowly turned his head to me and pointed at the window, "Course, every now and then we get a couple dogs fucking out there."

I thought it perhaps an attempt at a joke, but he seemed serious enough. I already wanted to leave but felt trapped somehow. I didn't want to upset him. "Um, last weekend I enrolled my aunt here," I began, "and..."

He interrupted with some irritation. "Enrolled?" he snorted, and then repeated louder, "ENROLLED? You mean *dumped off* don'tcha?"

I sought to mollify him. "Oh no," I gasped and quickly asked him to please keep his voice down.

"Why?" he retorted with loud indignity. "Everybody in here is ASLEEP." He turned to look at the room for effect. Not a soul budged. "See?" he asked, poking his thumb over his shoulder with vindication. "And even if they *can* hear, they don't care."

I tried a different approach. "Pardon me, it's just that Auntie Stephanie means so very much to me. But, well, she has become such a handful –"

Again he interrupted but this time with enthusiasm. "Stephanie? The new talent? Hey, she's a nice little piece." He chortled. "I guess she's a handful. I'd like ta getta handfulla those knockers –"

"Mr. Supreme!" I cut him off sharply.

"Just *Supreme* will do," he intoned with some irritation and a wave of his hand.

"Please sir, she's dear to me."

"Yeah, well, she's becoming a favorite of mine too," he said with what could almost pass for charm. "Can I wrangle an introduction from you?"

"Mr. Rotzinger –"

"Supreme."

I gave in. "OK, Supreme."

"That's better."

"I'm only trying to find out a bit about this place. You seem to know your way around."

He grunted disparagingly. "There's not much to know. Whadja say your name was?"

"Marvin."

"Well Marv – can I call you Marv? the food's OK." He thought for a bit.

"That's it?"

"Well, I'm not much for board games or bingo. I do like movies," he said, somewhat hopefully.

"Oh. How about the staff, how're they?"

"Fine, I mean, what can they do? They serve food and clean up after us. It ain't rocket science." His face darkened. He actually lowered his voice and leaned towards me. "See, you should know I shouldn't be here."

Of course, I thought, no one should be here.

Rotzinger prattled along. "It was the damn Palin-O'Donnell Administration did it, when Republicans controlled Congress, when they privatized everything – Social Security, then Medicare!" He fairly spat the words out. "Then the Department of Education, then the CIA, then Defense, then –"

I cut him off. "I know, I *know*. Everything, they privatized everything."

"Right, which maybe woulda been OK," he barreled on, "if the goddam terrorists hadna nuked Manhattan!! I lost my nest egg!!!"

"Yes, we all know about that," I empathized. There was an obligatory, reverent, shared silence between us – that recent attack had indeed been a bad day for our great nation. I tried to explain what I had never understood. "The stock market, it turned out, had been in some kind of weekend transition thing, hadn't quite gotten everything backed up right, things weren't nearly redundant enough. I lost a ton too."

He was indignant. "I thought cyber space was some kind of force field orbiting Earth."

"No," I softly corrected him, "it's on hardware in buildings." Some of which were vaporized. And, of course, New York City would be uninhabitable for the next century or so.

He was now wound up and spewing. "I was gonna retire to fucking TAHITI. I was a big guy; I ran shit; I ran BUSINESSES." He paused to let that sink in. "And now I'm stuck in this, this *institution*." Spittle flew from his flapping lips.

The silence returned as we pondered not only the national tragedy but the local one as well. He spoke first. "Why couldna the terrorists just hit those two lunatic babes in the White House? I'da been cool with that."

That administration had truly been a debacle from which there was no real return.

He still wasn't finished, "And I was *right wing* for Crissake – it was like gettin' kicked in the family jewels by your own duenna."

What was a duenna? What was I talking to?

"Marv, can you help me with something?"

"I can try."

"OK, how exactly did those two broads sell our Defense Department to China?"

I was forced to confess I'd been a bit busy the week that had happened and wasn't sure precisely how it had transpired. "It had something to do with the gazillions of dollars we owed them," I lamely replied. "I don't think we completely sold it."

"Well, OK," he acknowledged, "but answer me this. So China is like managing our entire armed forces capability, right?"

"Yes," I said, "I think so. And doing a darned good job of it, I might add."

"Well, OK," he repeated, "but what if China attacks us?"

"Um, I think that's when the Palin Codicil kicks in."

"What the hell is that? Marv, you put a codicil in a *will*!"

"Well, Palin never really leaned into the English language as you may recall, was somewhat imprecise in those waters. Very often words got in the way of what she was trying to say." He nodded but it was in exasperation. I went on, "I think it basically prohibits the Chinese from attacking us with our own military."

Rotz seemed lost. "Or else what?" he demanded.

"Um, I don't know."

"Precisely!" he shot back. "A military is the great OR ELSE. The last RESORT. The fucking HAMMER. What's to stop them? What, what, what…?" He waved his hands helplessly.

It was indeed a poser. I wasn't sure. "They were women –"

"Speaking of chicks," he interrupted, and turned to me knowingly, "at least we got some decent chicks here."

My worst fears were confirmed. It suddenly occurred to me that I wasn't quite sure of the reach and range of human sexuality these days, what with all those new hormonal enhancement drugs whizzing about. How bad had it gotten? Like it or not, I figured I was about to find out.

"Like old people fuck…" he was musing with disgust, "like we do it poorly. Who came up with that one? What a pathetic simile that is."

I wondered how had he come up with a word like *simile*, but he was off on this new tear.

"What an insult, like old people fuck. How dare they?" He was sincere. "We fuck GREAT!" he exclaimed, pushing an arthritic and crooked index finger into the air for effect. "We have *learned* how to fuck, we got experience. We take entire AFTERNOONS for sex. We fall asleep fucking and then wake up still fucking. Lemme tell ya, it's TERRIFIC. We got TIME!" As an aside he added, "Of course, I do have to carry a tube of lube around, but what the hell…" he paused to inhale, "there's nothing *else* to do here."

I was apoplectic. What I had done to dear Auntie S? I pictured a large, well-appointed room somewhere in the bowels of Peaceful Pastures stocked with all manner of sexual devices, lotions and vibrators and harnesses and manacles and chains and immense beds and mirrors and a communal Jacuzzi and hi-def recording devices, a dungeon where orgies were routine. It was unnerving beyond measure. Somehow, Rotzinger had sensed my disapproval. His tone softened, he sought to draw me in. "C'mon Marv, you ever screwed a babe when she was asleep?" he asked.

I was speechless. My mind engaged… OK, I assumed Deirdre faked an orgasm on occasion. Did she fake sleeping, or being awake? In any event, it was a painful reminder that foreplay back at our house had pretty much devolved into me begging.

"Well," he pressed on, "did you ever get laid while you were asleep?"

"Um, er, ah… how would I even know…?"

He cut me off. "Then don't knock it till ya TRIED it!"

I felt trapped. My heart was racing. I stood up and sat down. Synapses were short-circuiting.

Rotzinger's grating voice brought me back to the picture window. "Nobody gets pregnant here!" he spouted with enthusiasm, "An' there's no VDs either. An' nobody tells tales outta school because nobody can *remember* anything. Every date is a *first* date." Again the finger in the air.

I was stricken dumb. I had to get Stephanie out of there. But how? Deirdre would kill me. What would I tell her?

I decided to try to change the subject. I asked Rotzinger about the *Teutons* pennant. It worked.

"The College," he answered simply.

"What college?" I asked.

"You didn't see the College?" he said.

"No."

"South enda town. Nowadays they call it Castle Cyber University. Used to be Einfahrt College."

"Ein-fahrt?" I had trouble with the word.

"Yeah, Einfahrt. That's German for *entrance*. The idea was that this place was the gateway for farm kids to get into the world. Used to be a big deal around here, the College. They had classrooms and labs and nice buildings and dorms and everything, playing fields. Lotsa students."

"What happened?"

"Well, it's still there, but it's all computers these days. Some kinda

15

academic make-over. They got thousands of students, but none of 'em are here. They're all over the place, Somalia or Mongolia for all I know. It's just computer courses. You can probably get a doctorate in Nuclear Physics from them. I wouldn't trust it though."

What had I fallen into?

"There's maybe three actual people at work over there, manning the machines. That's it."

"Einfahrt is not a great name," I observed drily. "Why not Lionfart?"

"Oh, I know. We kept trying to change it. The story was that when they named the place it came down to Einfahrt or Zitpuke and after much deliberation they went with Einfahrt. Castle Cyber University is an improvement, CCU. But back in the day though, we were the Einfahrt Teutons. Aw what the hell, it had a nice ring to it. And it was a storied institution, went back to the mid-1800s."

"You went there?"

"Didn't have much of a choice. I came from a town near here, couldn't afford to go anywhere far away. Good ol' EZ EC. It was cheap and close to home. Most of the kids were from small towns and farms in Iowa."

"Four-year school?"

"In theory, yes."

"What was it like?"

"Well, very German. And Christian."

"That doesn't sound too promising," I offered.

"Bite your tongue," Rotz leapt to the defense, shooting back as quickly as a 90-plus-year-old man can shoot back. "The best years of my life!"

"Really?" I wondered aloud, considering the abysmal state of Burgfort.

"We were young, asshole," he retorted. "We had YOUTH. And we played FOOTBALL." He raised both spindly arms as if to signal a touchdown.

"Oh, sorry," I said.

"What's to be sorry about football?" he attacked. "Football is stellar!" Saliva splattered everywhere.

"OK, OK," I granted him by way of apology. Geez, I needed a splash guard to talk to this guy.

"And we had a House," he intoned, with a sudden sense of reverence.

I remembered what the custodian had said about Rotzinger and the house he was always rambling on about. This must be it. What was it called? Carla?

"Cotta House," his tone was worshipful. His head tilted back, his eyes slowly closed, and he was blissfully at rest.

I left quickly and quietly.

But that old man had gotten to me. My mind was processing on the ride back home. Things were all upside down, problems needed solving. I couldn't run from them. Like an accident on the side of a road, the first inclination is to turn away, but the blood and guts, the gore, somehow drew you in. I had to return as soon as possible.

Nothing is easy. Write that down.

3. The Buffalo

I decided against so much as mentioning Rotzinger to Deirdre. She'd only be angry, and what was I to do anyway? There were professionals working at the assisted living complex, they knew their business. Surely they appreciated and understood whatever situations were afoot and were doing their best with them. What more could I do? I'd be in the way is all.

Yet the first Saturday morning in August saw me in the van heading for Burgfort out of concern for poor, trusting Auntie S. The idea of someone like Rotzinger possessing her bothered me for some reason. I had to be there.

Upon arrival, the informal reports I got from the Peaceful Pastures staff were excellent. Auntie Stephanie was fitting right in, had made many friends, and was bubbly as could be. She was a regular live wire, flitting about, adhering to all the rules, never a problem.

She was also never in her room. I wondered for an instant if I were being gamed. Maybe Auntie S had run off in the first week and everyone was only pretending she was there. What would I know? Payments would keep automatically arriving from the retirement account I'd set up for her, and everyone would be fine with it. The inmates – er patients, or whatever you called them – got very few visitors. I could be expected to stop dropping by in a short while. My aunt was one less mouth to feed...

So it was with great relief that I caught a glimpse of her walking down a corridor. "Auntie Steph!" I yelled.

She looked and saw me and said breezily, "Hi. Just a sec. Be right back." And continued on her way.

I knew her well enough to know she would not be right back. She would forget. Rather than chase her, I headed for the community room. I'd decided to stay close to Rotzinger because I figured he'd tell me if he'd done anything to Auntie Stephanie, even brag about it. The man was that brazen. I found him in his usual spot on his usual couch, but the woman beside him was different. Sadly, however, their hands were in each other's laps.

As I walked towards him, he saw me coming and slid into his electric cart, leaving the woman sleeping by herself, her head laid back on a cushion and her mouth wide open. I grabbed a folding chair and followed as he threaded his way silently over to the rear picture window.

I sat down and asked in a coy, playful way, pointing to the woman, "What does she have that the other one didn't?"

"Parkinson's," he replied.

It was beginning to dawn on me that there might still be wheels turning in that bald head of his.

I surely didn't want to talk with him about Steph, it being a sore and uncomfortable subject for me. The only other option at hand was that House. I asked him if I could tender a few questions. "By all means," he answered, and leaned back as a counselor might, open and agreeable.

"What was Cotta House exactly?" I began.

"It was an off-campus house," he answered. "It was a complete rip in the fabric."

"How did it work?"

His response was immediate. "It didn't work – that's the whole point."

"Well then, OK, how *didn't* it work?"

Rotzinger thought for a bit, and then said, "The Buffalo."

This seemed to explain everything, at least so far as he was concerned.

"What was the Buffalo?" I carefully asked.

"Fred," he simply said. "We also called him Ferd Berfel, I have no idea why."

"Fred and Ferd is confusing."

"Oh Marv, we're just gettin' started with confusion. There was no shortage of crazy bastards floating through Cotta. Pay close attention from here on out."

I blinked.

"Now, we called Fred *Buff* for short," he explained. "He liked Buffalos, felt some strange kinship to them. Even during college he started growing a series of thick, auburn beards. He put on weight over the years and retained his leonine pile of curly brown hair. He came to sort of *look* like a buffalo. He was a center on the football team, which meant he was powerful and agile, the anchor of the offensive line. He was squat – you want that in a center. He was from Montana."

"Wow," I exclaimed, "long ways away."

"Actually, no," he corrected me, "Montana, Illinois, a little town. His dad had a factory there, made custom boilers."

"Boilers?"

"Yeah, the contraptions that heat buildings. There's a lotta money in those things, ya know. Imagine heating a skyscraper."

"Oh, OK."

"The Buffalo was the full flowering of Cotta House. He embodied the place. Now, Cotta had been around for at least two decades or more before we got there. For better or worse, the traditions of the House had been shaped prior to his arrival, but they just kinda coalesced when he moved in. He had an enormous capacity for mirth, for fun. He loved to laugh, was the prince of good times. There was this subliminal sentiment, never really discussed, that told every Cotta man that in Berfel, the Buddha had landed."

"Wow. He must have been something then."

"And then some," Rotz mused. "He had no sense of aftermath. He was his father's only son and had been indulged (as had most of us), so he never really seemed to have to pay for anything. He never worried about punishment of any kind."

I was searching for an appropriate question. "What kinda stuff did he do?"

Once again, Rotz closed his eyes in thought. When he had downloaded his response, they opened and he began, "The Buffalo had a Barracuda…"

"A fish?" I blurted with surprise.

Rotz shook his head in disbelief. I was constantly disappointing him, it seemed, which bothered me. I had to take more care when commenting. Somehow, he was making me feel like an idiot.

"A car, Merv. Plymouth made them. They were sporty. They had big engines, the Valiant generation of Slant-6s, and they were the first of the fastbacks. They didn't have a trunk, you lifted the hatchback and there was your load space. They had four seats, two front and two back, but you could put the back seats down to increase the load space. You could stretch out and sleep back there, if you were short."

"Oh," I said, wondering how I could have been so dumb as to not know that.

"Buff drove that car like there was no tomorrow, which, in a perfect world – one with consequences – there would not have been. How he never managed to kill himself and his passengers on some lonely blacktop is beyond me. But it was part of his beer mystique."

"He drove drunk?" I asked with a touch of amazement.

"Marv," Rotz replied, "back then, the *designated driver* was the guy who owned the vehicle, whatever shape he was in."

I shook my head.

"I know," he commiserated, "such were the times." He leaned back. "I remember one cold winter's Friday night when we'd been at a basketball game at Calvin College. Now, Calvin, being a Christian school like Einfahrt, was a big rival. It was an hour or two away. Back before cable TV and the fucking Internets," he chewed those words with a touch of enmity, "we actually went out and did stuff. There was this thing called *life*, which existed in the place cyber space has come to occupy and which is now called life *style*. We didn't have video games, *life* was our video game."

I leaned forward in my chair.

"Anyway, the Teutons had been victorious, we were in the Barracuda, Buff was drinking a can of beer and driving us back to Burgfort after the game, and there was a blizzard descending. It wasn't considered wise to tell the Buffalo how to do anything, much less drive. He had this stubborn streak which would respond to suggestions about how to modify his behavior with an intensification of said behavior."

"That doesn't sound good," I volunteered.

"It wasn't," said Rotz matter-of-factly, "and Berfel was in a hurry. We were sliding all over the road, going 80 miles an hour. Somehow, we made it back to town, where Ferd proceeded to run all four red lights on Main Street, at speed, blasting his way to the campus. In retrospect, it's hard to see how we could have *not* come under the watchful eyes of the local constabulary. Inevitably, back while we'd been negotiating the Maple River bridge, we'd picked up an escort, red lights flashing and siren wailing.

"This in no way served to deter Fred's agenda. He simply fish-tailed a neat donut and headed back in the direction of the cop car, passing it and turning down a side street.

"Good god," I found myself saying, "and you guys just let that go?"

"Well, there were many obscenities aired at volume as I recall. But then we were all drunk, so it was sorta like the pot calling the kettle black. We were mostly praying, I think. Berfel managed to find a back route to Einfahrt and parked the car in the gravel driveway next to Cotta, where we all immediately jumped out and scattered. I took a moment to kiss the snowy ground, then ran to the house next door where the basketball players lived and joined a dandy party that was building in their basement, waiting as they were for their victorious house brothers' return.

"Not five minutes later, I was called up to the front door to find a Burgfort cop in uniform waiting to talk with me. He asked who the white Barracuda belonged to. I gave him Buffalo's name. He seemed to already know that. He asked where Fred was. I told him I didn't know, which was the truth. He wondered if I'd check in Cotta House. So we headed next door. While passing the Barracuda, the cop's partner, a young and enthusiastic moron, put his ear to the hood and announced, 'This car's warm; this car's been driven.' The lead cop looked at him as if to say, 'No shit Sherlock,' and we continued to Cotta. The cop wanted to remain on the porch in the snowy cold, I suppose because he had no warrant, but I invited him into the front hallway and went to pretend to look for Buff.

"I made a great show of opening all three bedroom doors on the first floor and reported a lack of success; the place was deserted. I went upstairs and picked a door, opening and closing it a few times while yelling downstairs, 'No sign of him up here.' Before descending, on a whim, I opened the door to the second floor hall closet and there sat the Buffalo, half-hidden by hanging coats, a big smile on his face, drinking a beer and eating a peanut butter and jelly sandwich. I closed the door, walked back down the stairs, and told the officer that there was no sign of Ferd in the House. He told me to tell him when I saw him to please come to the police station on Monday to talk. I assured him I would."

"So the Buffalo was toast, I guess," I said.

Rotz looked at me with disbelief. I'd screwed up again. "Well, they had him, didn't they?" I pled without confidence.

"Hardly," Rotz countered. "They had no idea who'd been driving the car. Buff went to the police station and denied everything. End of case."

"He just lied?"

"Of course he lied. Believe me, the Commandments were thoroughly visited upon us – we knew all ten. There is no 'Thou shalt not lie.' Ya can't have a successful marriage without lies. All's fair in love and war – and police."

"What about testifying?" I asked.

"Well, yeah," he explained, "ya can't bear false witness, that's Commandment Eight as I recall. But the Buffalo wasn't under oath."

"How did he ever manage to graduate?" I asked.

"No problem," Rotz said, "a distinguished history major. But in general, I'm not sure who all graduated and who didn't. I know *I* did.

There was often a question as to who was actually even enrolled in school as opposed to those living there simply because they had no place else to go."

"Um," was all I could think to say.

Rotz could see I was having trouble comprehending. "Well lemme tell you about Joy's," he began anew.

"Joy's," I repeated.

"Joy's," he went on, "fucking echo in here?" He looked at me quizzically, then looked around in what I took to be an attempt at jest. When I didn't laugh, he went on, "Joy's was the local greasy spoon. The most famous truck stop in Iowa."

"What made it so special?" I asked.

"The grill," he immediately replied. "I've never seen another like it. Had to have been custom-made. It wasn't a dry grill, it was about two or three inches deep and filled with molten grease, pure grease. Every morning, about two A.M., they drained the used grease and cleaned the grill. Then they took a big can of fresh, solid, white lard and ladled a load onto the grill, where it melted quickly and filled it up. They made burgers and pork tenderloins in there, and after a few hours, the original grease had the added flavor of the grease from all that other stuff. By morning, wow, their food tasted great.

"The specialty of the house, the *pièce de résistance*, was the Egg-Cheese Sandwich. It really was only a cheese omelet on a hamburger bun, but it was made in all that fragrant grease. First the cook would crack an egg, one-handed, and drop it into a white coffee mug. Then he'd take a fork – always the same mug and fork, no rinsing – and stir the egg in the mug. Then he'd dump the scrambled egg into the grease, where it would completely disappear. Magically, however, in a half-minute or so, as it coagulated and cooked, it would reappear, this yellowish-white circle floating on the grease."

"OMG," I managed.

"Hey, they were toothsome. Now listen. When the egg was done, the cook would put a slice of American cheese on it and fold it over. Then he would put the top of a bun on it, holding it with his left hand while he took a spatula and lifted the thing from the grill with his right, pushing the spatula against the sandwich, which would effectively drain the grease back into the grill."

"That just sounds awful," I said.

"I know, it does. To the uninitiated, the mere sight of such a thing was on occasion a bridge too far. They'd rescind their order. I mean, the grease literally poured from the sandwich. Then the cook put it on the bottom of the bun and served it. You could get pickles and raw onions if you wanted them, and of course there was ketchup and mustard. God it was good. What I wouldn't give for one of those right now."

I didn't know what to say.

"Joy's never closed," he went on. "It was crackerbox, just a counter with about eight stools and a coupla small tables behind it, each of those sat two. Yet there was always someone eating there. They did a huge carry-out business. Their stuff was delicious, the best ever. On weekend nights, the place was packed.

"One Saturday night, I walked in about 1 A.M. and Ferd Berfel was sitting at the counter waiting for his food. He was completely shit-faced, a dumbass smile and eyes that didn't quite focus. He had a cigarette in his mouth that wasn't lit. His left elbow was on the counter, and he had a book of matches in his left hand, which his forehead was leaning on. He tore a match loose with his right hand and struck it across the matchbook. And it lit. But he was slow to take it away from the book, so all the other matches ignited. He was sitting there smiling at me and his hand was on fire. It took a while for the pain to register. When he realized what was happening, he pounded the fire out on the counter. And just laughed. He was lucky his hair didn't ignite."

I was mulling over this new incongruity when Rotz started to speak again, as if attempting to explain the totality of the climate in which all of this was possible.

"Ferd was not, um, unattractive," he said, delicately, "he could be considered 'dashing'. I have no idea what women see in men, but he had a straight, rakish nose, doe eyes, and a killer smile. And what with his dad being of some means and possessed with a generosity imparted to his son, there was this aura around him. Fred always carried large amounts of cash in a roll, which was uncharacteristic for that time and place. Chicks found him cute, maybe even irresistible. He got more action by accident than the rest of us got on purpose.

"And one late night, he had a coed we called Mickey in the Barracuda and was parked in a forested make-out spot by the river. They were necking heavily in the front seats. Ferd had probably even gotten to the groping portion of the skirmish. But what with bucket seats being then as now encumbrances in such encounters, the Buffalo had thoughtfully put the back seats down, in advance, in case Mickey would turn out to be in heat. Since that had, in fact, come to pass, he asked her if she'd like to go back to the rear of the car and stretch out.

"'No,' she replied, 'I wanna stay up here with you.'"

4. Cotta House

It was one of those stealth non-sequiturs that builds. The more I thought about it, the funnier it got. As I was digesting it, Rotzinger excused himself and drove off, expertly negotiating the maze of furniture to the men's room in the hallway at the far end of the parlor. There, anticipating his arrival, a large sliding door opened to his approach and closed after he motored through it.

He was gone an inordinately long time, leaving me to think. First, I began to wonder what he could possibly be doing in there, but that led down a fairly distasteful corridor, a train of thought I quickly dropped in favor of mulling on what I had just heard from him. It was fascinating for some reason, I guess because it was so foreign to me.

My musings were interrupted by his return. I was encouraged to discover he had remembered I was sitting waiting for him. I had considered, in his absence, the possibility that he might have forgotten me completely by the time he had put the finishing touches on whatever chaos he had imparted to the men's room. But no, there he was, in position by the picture window as if he'd never left. "You asked about Cotta House," he said.

Well, I hadn't in a while. I had only been trying to humor him. It didn't matter. I was going to hear about it anyway. It was to be the price I paid for proximity.

"Think of Cotta House," he began sternly, as though lecturing, "as a jumbo cluster fuck."

"How do you mean that?" I asked.

"It took a very large number of things all going wrong at the same time to enable it," he replied.

"Oh. Like what?"

"Geez, well…" He put his fingers to his forehead, was a study in concentration for a few moments before speaking. "I guess we can start with the Germanicism of it all, the Germanness. The German thing. Whatever you wanna call it. See, the 20th century was not a real good one for Germans. There was that colonialism misadventure, all those dumb alliances and treaties. When the first big war broke out, Germany's allies turned out to be dog waste, pretty much, pussies. Bad choices."

He grew a bit more animated as he warmed to his subject. "Then Hitler came along a decade or so later. And then the Holocaust. Bad shit there. World War II wasn't a great time to be a German in America. Come to think of it, it wasn't a great time to be a German in Germany either. I'm not sure it was good to be a German *anywhere*, but in America anyway, Germans tended to just shut up and try to disappear. That was the response: duck and cover. Stay the hell outta the way. Make no waves. See it through.

"Now the Italians, I mean, they're shameless. They screwed up their 20th century as bad as the Germans – left Germany hanging – and you also got the Mafia thing with them. Doesn't matter, Italians are constantly yellin' around about themselves and havin' Columbus Day parades and glorifying lasagna and all that shit. Chest pumping for no good reason. Not Germans. They got quiet, so as not to call attention. Germans hid, which was the appropriate response.

"A lotta Germans even changed their names, or anglicized them. My dad changed our name. The original name was *Ratzinger,* spelled R-a-t-z. Meant 'from Ratzing'. And a *ratzkeller* is something like a basement. Dad didn't want to look like a rat, I guess. He changed its spelling to R-o-t-z, which is how it's pronounced in German. Doesn't seem like much of an improvement to me, but those were strange times."

I could tell Rotzinger had put some thought into this. It seemed a bit half-baked, but it was earnest and, at the very least, entertaining. Another county heard from.

"So you're German," I assumed.

"Careful," came the rejoinder, "my mom was Danish, thank heavens. My saving grace, the great Dane."

"Oh," I said. I hadn't realized any of this still mattered to anyone. Obviously it did to Rotz.

"Germans are schtuppy," he added, "and by the way, there was a Pope named Ratzinger, with an *a*."

"I thought they were all named Pope names."

"Well, yeah, he took a Pope name after he was elected, but this guy was a German. He was in there at the beginning of the century. Came after JP 2. Was involved in that big, ongoing sex scandal, as I recall. Can you believe those fuckin' Catholics?" he smiled and paused for effect. "Italians again," he sighed, then brightened. "Germans, by contrast, are Lutherans. So are Danes." Another arthritic finger in the air.

I was reflecting on the German reformation thing when he interrupted.

"Anyway, the College stuck to itself, didn't air any dirty laundry. Grinned and bore it. The town did too." He stopped to think. I wondered if he were nodding off.

"Um, Supreme?"

He snapped back to his narrative. "Another component was beer. Germans drink beer. They make good beer and they drink it. Immense quantities of it. Heart-pounding quantities. It's a tradition. I had an uncle used to say, 'You can live on beer, but you can't live on soda pop.' He was right. In fact, come to think of it, about the only German tradition you got in America is Oktoberfest. That's the only time it's OK to be German. God did we drink beer at Cotta. Ridiculous, silly, insane amounts." Another pause.

I felt like I should have been taking notes.

"Then you had the Christian thing," he continued. "That was a kind of backwards facilitator."

"What do you mean?"

"Christians are bent," he stated flatly. "Being a Lutheran college, we had all these guys running around who were pre-theological students, determined to head to a seminary and be pastors. We had a buncha ministers on campus as well. We had *church* on campus. There was this constant theme, sin and forgiveness, Christian charity, like that."

"You mean anything you did was OK?" I asked, starting to get it.

"Exactly," he responded. "The crazier you were, the more you were supported, as a soul to save if nothing else. You were a project. You were embraced in the community of saints. Kinda like a free pass to fuck up."

"Um…"

"And there was this housing shortage on campus. Einfahrt had grown rapidly thanks to the GI Bill, was up to around 1,500 students, and there weren't enough dorms. Well, the College had been buying up all the houses that surrounded it so it could tear them down and build more classrooms and shit. And it was like all those weather-beaten houses had been erected at the same time by the same people. They were old, two-story, white structures with basements. And attics. And covered front porches. Simple. One blueprint for all, if there even was a blueprint. They looked the same. Nothing fancy, just basic shelter for an average family.

"So anyway, the College started using them for housing. Now, they kept the girls in dorms where they could better ride herd on them – back then the girls had hours and had to sign in and out of the dorms at night. Unbelievably sexist in retrospect. But the College had started putting the guys in off-campus houses. And one of those was named *Cotta*. We got to invite in who we wanted to live there."

"They were fraternities then," I said, trying to help.

"Christ no," Rotzinger cut me off. "That was another thing that went wrong. They weren't fraternities. If they'da been fraternities, there woulda been national codes of conduct, dues to pay. There woulda been some kinda framework, some accountability. But the houses were too small to be frat houses. And we didn't like the sound of 'fraternity' anyway. Sounded too swishy, too East Coast, too fancy-schmantzy. Sounded expensive. Sounded like rules."

"No accountability? Whattaya mean?"

"None we could immediately see. They couldn't very well throw us out, they desperately needed the money. Every warm body paid tuition."

I was starting to get it.

"Speaking of rules," he went on, "then you had the Sixties. Jesus Christ, the Sixties."

"Oh yeah," I offered, recalling dimly. "What were they like?"

"Well, ya hadda be there for the Sixties, and if you remembered 'em, ya weren't. Steve Stills said that."

It sounded like a riddle. *Stills* was a name I wasn't familiar with. "That was when this drug thing started, right?"

"The Sixties were a lot more than just drugs."

"Lotta drugs at Cotta?" I ventured.

"Shit no. Burgfort was isolated, hardly a crossroads of any kind, off the map. I mean, we heard about all these exotic drugs, LSD and all that, and we had dirt weed growing wild out in the ditches of Iowa, but we never did any drugs. There weren't any around to do. We just drank beer."

I wanted to point out that alcohol was a drug, but he was off on another tangent like a bloodhound after a scent.

"The great mantra of the Sixties was *no rules*. Vietnam triggered that. Every campus worth its salt back then had protests about that dumbass war. We had 'em at Einfahrt."

I was trying to remember that 20th century history course I'd had back in college, but it was fuzzy. "Why were there protests?" I managed, stalling for time.

Rotz thought a moment. "Damn near every guy on campus coulda been drafted." He caught himself, "Oh, maybe not yanked right outta college, but when they graduated or got expelled or quit. Every single one of us had to confront the prospect of gettin' hauled over to balmy Southeast Asia and gettin' killed. Or maimed."

"Geez."

"Then there was the Civil Rights Movement. It said it's OK to break bad laws, which it was and still is. We self-servingly figured the draft was a bad law. And the women bought into that shit too because they were, like, an oppressed minority. And the Pill came along about then, with outcomes that, looking back, were entirely predictable. So, it was a complete circle jerk."

I'd had the Sixties explained to me ever since I could remember, but never more succinctly. This version actually made some sense. In the back of my head was the concept of the *prairie populist*, but I wasn't sure where it had come from, and I wasn't certain what it was, exactly. Maybe this was it though, maybe Supreme was the prairie populist.

He continued. "It was a total breakdown of authority. Inner cities were burning, draft cards were burning, bras were burning." He thought for a moment. "I kinda liked that last one."

I chuckled.

"The older generation, the fucking *Greatest Generation* guys, they were thrown back on their heels. They had this attitude like, 'Well, we served in Europe and the Pacific, now it's your turn.' What they forgot about was that ever since our generation had been in elementary school, we'd been flooded with newsreel movies in classrooms about World War II, grainy black and white footage of real war, not some glossy Hollywood patriotic shit, but guys actually gettin' mowed down hittin' the beaches and crawlin' around in jungles. And most of those little fourth-graders were watching that shit and thinking – I know *I* was – 'War doesn't look like as much fun as I thought.'

"And so when they came at us with this draft shit, there was a collective national juvenile sentiment that said, 'Fuck you, I ain't gonna fight your stupid war.' Something about the law of unintended consequences… they thought all that war documentary stuff would make us appreciate what they'd done. And we did. But it had basically scared the piss out of us. We just didn't wanna do it."

"OK," I allowed, "I'll give you that. But why then didn't anyone protest the Iraq War, that second one, after the Towers were hit, the one that bankrupted the nation?"

"Well," and Rotz had this answer on the tip of his tongue, "the old guys, the money, fixed all that shit from the Sixties. They reasoned, correctly it turned out, that the draft was the problem. If you had a volunteer army, nobody would give a damn because they were all mercenaries in uniform, basically. The big money guys were that cynical. They saw the Sixties as anarchy, and that gave them great pause, so they moved to fix things. They figured the problem was the open exchange of information, *democracy* as it were – a free press. And in the '70s they bought the goddam media. They bought the radio stations and the TV stations and the newspapers and magazines. Just bought 'em.

"So, you could have some goody two-shoes liberal journalism major from outta Radcliffe determined to find some crusade to pounce on and make a name for herself, and that was OK. They could let her cute little leftist socialist notions dink around in some barrio, helping poor people and what have you, but when it came time for the big-league editorials, the money was doing the talking."

"Fascinating," I murmured.

"Which is why when a normal media shoulda been crying foul at the wars of choice Bush junior started, beginning of the century, there was no real media to lead the charge. All the reporters were *embedded*, in with the troops. The establishment gave 'em front-row seats to the carnage. They got to be big hairy 'war correspondents' without any real risk. They were riding around in fucking tanks and shit. They weren't objective, they were cheerleaders."

And suddenly, in my head, tumblers clicked. "What'd you major in?" I asked, already suspecting the answer.

"History," he said, stopping to catch his breath.

Having worn out on the Sixties, I brought him back to what I'd inexplicably become interested in, that House. "Where'd they get the name, Cotta?" I asked.

"We think it was some kinda dormitory in Germany. We heard

Martin Luther lived there for a while. We consider Luther the first Cotta man."

"How many guys lived there?"

His reply was instant. "Fifteen at a time. There were four rooms upstairs, two guys each. Three rooms downstairs, one a 3-man, one on the back porch. One bathroom upstairs with a tub. A shower in the basement. A kitchen and a living room."

"That was it?"

"That was it."

"Fifteen guys shared one bathroom, one toilet?"

"On warm nights we peed out the windows."

I blinked. "What else?" I asked.

"What else what?"

"What else went wrong."

He thought a bit. "Iowa," he finally said.

"What about Iowa?"

"It's not very cosmopolitan. It's mostly farms and little towns. Most of the guys at Einfahrt were from farms and towns." He said it as though that explained something.

"And so…?" I didn't quite get it.

"Well, they're what Molière called *bon bourgeois*, good-hearted peasants. They were very trusting. They'd do anything. They had no standard of comparison. Like, one night over beers in our room, some big farm kid asked what he could do to get into the House. He really wanted in. My roomie Potz said it wasn't lead-pipe cinch, but if the kid could put his head through one of our walls, that might impress the guys next time they voted. Potz even drew a target on a wall with a felt marker. Without hesitation, the guy first carefully set his beer down, then he ran head first into the wall."

"What happened?" I asked in amazement.

"Potz had drawn the target over a support beam, a two by four or something. You could see the vertical row of nails if you looked. The kid bounced off…"

"Geez, was he OK?"

34

"Seemed fine, wanted to try again, seemed a bit embarrassed at not getting it the first time."

"You let him?"

"Let him? Guys were encouraging him, cheering him on. He bounced off again and they were telling him he almost had it, like, just one more charge would do it and so on... until he finally knocked himself out cold."

"Did he get hurt?"

"Bad headache, stiff neck. Otherwise none the worse for wear."

"That's remarkable. That was cruel you know. He could have broken his neck."

"Maybe, I dunno. It was funny."

"You took advantage," I said, evenly.

"I suppose. I'm sorry. We were bullet-proof back then. We just didn't think about injuries much."

"Why?"

Rotzinger took a deep breath. He seemed at last to have arrived at the heart of the matter. "Cotta House was the football house," he said reverently. "Football breeds a special kind of, oh, *individual.* Football is combat. Football is war. Football is lunacy. Football is a culture. It's really not a very safe thing to do."

"Then why did you do it?"

"Because it was so much fun! It satisfies a body in so many ways, on so many levels." Supreme and the story line were now one. Saliva once again splattered; he gesticulated sharply, underscoring the points as he made them. "It's the savage physical contact, the primal nature of the sport. It's really the perfect American game, if you think about it, insofar as it's all about the premeditated, violent takeover of territory, of land. You gain ground inch by inch, yard by yard. You hurt people. You murder them in metaphor."

It occurred to me that I had never really talked with a football player before. I had to admit, it was intriguing. I asked what position he played.

"I came from high school as a quarterback. I ran the show. But, turned

35

out the Teutons already had a quarterback, a good passer, Speckle. And I was big and sort of fast, had good hands, so they made me a tight end."

"What is that, exactly? I mean, I've heard the term…"

"Well, a tight end is a pass receiver who blocks. He has to do both. Wide receivers and flankers are fast, sprinter types, they go downfield deep a lot to catch long bombs. A tight end is more the lineman, stockier."

"I played a little basketball when I was younger," I said. "Is football like basketball?"

Rotz thought a bit, then replied, "Not really."

"Um," I said. "How is it different?"

Rotz looked at me, pursed his lips, and for the first time seemed to approve, as if I'd finally asked a worthy question.

"There's always room on a football field," he said at last, "for a coupla guys who have completely lost their heads."

5. Rotz's Room

The next Saturday morning, Deirdre wanted me to help her straighten out the pile of junk that had accumulated over the years in our basement's back room. I begged off, telling her I needed to go check up on Auntie Stephanie. She did not appreciate this, was testy about it. Her anger escalated into an the argument which was titanic, unlike any set-to I could recall having with her since before we were married.

She erupted, raining down epithets and threats on me. I couldn't imagine where it all had come from, like she'd been storing it up for quite a while. It was such a surprise I couldn't do much of anything but stand there like a whipped animal and absorb it. I had no comeback in my defense, had nothing to say. She was especially unkind to Aunt Stephanie, for reasons I couldn't figure out, Stephanie being out of the house. I'd been so busy with transitioning my aunt to the Complex I guess I'd lost track of my wife. Obviously, her needs weren't being met. But part of that misunderstanding was not knowing what her needs exactly were anymore.

I sat there in silence, head down, and let the rage blow over. When she was finished, one thing was very clear – I had to get out of the house. I was almost immediately on the road to Peaceful Pastures. As the van negotiated the journey, I was trying to figure out what had gone wrong.

It occurred to me that I had told my wife a complete lie. Maybe she sensed that.

I wasn't going to see Auntie S, I was going to see Rotzinger.

Steph had become so caught up with her new friends in the nursing home she didn't need me in the slightest, and if she hadn't already completely forgotten I even existed in the first place, surely at some point in the near future I would become a blank gap on her memory coil.

But a fascination with Rotzinger was growing. He was a doorway to a world I never knew existed, and I wanted to learn more about it. In the back of my head, the cloud of a book was beginning to coalesce. I wondered what other revelations were lurking in that mysterious domicile called Cotta House.

I arrived to find him on his customary sofa in the big parlor, alone this time, as if expecting me. Routine was creeping into the program. I typically arrived around 10 A.M. and left at lunch. The staff had hinted to me from the outset about the Saturday afternoon community *nap fests* that were so predictable as to almost be an event on the weekly schedule.

The basic elements of Cotta House had been laid out. Indeed, the old fellow had done a fine job of delineating them. But I had trouble framing them in context, figuring out how they meshed together, the chemistry and behaviors resulting from a combination of no rules, a German beer ethic, a Christian college, the Sixties, Iowa, a heap of testosterone, and football. I wondered what could possibly have been so special about it.

Then there was Rotzinger himself. Try as I might, I found myself liking him, a fairly ghastly and even disturbing outcome, considering the nature of the man. In spite of his advanced years, he was not rumpled. He wore crisp, pressed blue jeans exclusively, and either T-shirts or light sweatshirts. As for shoes, I had noticed several pair, all Guccis, whether slippers or casual footwear.

His eyes were clear and blue. His general manner was uncomfortably commanding, but one might expect that from any CEO, especially one with Hun genes. His voice was nasal, a kind of honk, like that of a goose but not unpleasant. The rasp had doubtless developed over the years, but the basic sound was still a compelling instrument. And when discussing Cotta, he became delightfully animated, even entertaining. That subject seemed to transform him. His eyes would twinkle. I had watched him grow visibly, almost miraculously, in stature when speaking of his beloved House. His voice had become stronger, and he evidenced a sense of purpose, however absurd.

It occurred to me that I might have stumbled upon a master storyteller. I wondered if he had ever written anything. While the general vibe of the nursing home was of a sort of worn out, resigned mess spilling everywhere, in Rotzinger there was a kind of wacky order. He didn't waste words, in fact he spoke directly and clearly. On the subject of Cotta House, at least, he was methodical. There was a stunning clarity to it all. I figured he had perhaps explained the place many times.

After exchanging greetings and pleasantries with him, I began to ask a series of questions which had come to me over the course of the past week. Chief among them was a general curiosity regarding the Cotta residents. Thus far I'd only met Supreme and Buffalo. Who were the others and what were they like?

Rotz responded by inviting me to his room. Frankly, I didn't want to go, figuring it probably smelled bad. But no sooner had he told me to follow him than he took off in his cart at high speed, and it was all I could do to keep up with the little flesh-colored pennant as he whipped down the halls, finally darting into an open door. I entered a moment later, a bit out of breath.

I had expected clutter. Instead, his side of the room was neat as a pin, and what odor there was seemed mildly antiseptic and pleasant. He shared the place with a man who was still in bed against the far wall.

"Hey Sid," he yelled, "wake up! We got company." Then he looked at me and chuckled.

Sid didn't move.

Rotz turned to him and shouted louder. "Sid, dammit, up and at 'em." He waited. Sid still didn't move.

"Holy shit," Rotz muttered under his breath. Then he looked to me, "Hey Marv, do me a favor, go check him for a pulse."

At first I thought he was joking. When I realized what I was being asked to do, I stopped in my tracks. Rotz got out of his cart, sat on his precisely-made bed, and looked up at me. "Go ahead," he encouraged, "he won't bite."

"That's what I'm afraid of," I answered, moving tentatively over to where the old man lay under his covers. I noticed he didn't seem to be breathing. I could see his face in profile against his pillow. His mouth was open, frozen open it seemed. His head was blue. "Um, Rotz," I carefully began, "I think he might be, ah…um…"

"Dead?" Rotz finished for me with indignation.

"Yeah," was all I could say while backing away from the body.

"Jesus Christ!" Rotz exclaimed. He made a fist and slammed the bottom of it against the big red emergency button on the wall by his headboard. "Time these bastards," he commanded.

"Excuse me?" I asked, momentarily confused. I'd never been around a corpse before.

"Put a watch on 'em. See how long it takes somebody to get here."

I checked my iWristBingle and we waited. While Rotz stewed on his bed, I walked around, looking at the room. There were many black and white photographs on the walls, all straight, even dusted. In them, young men wore sweatshirts with the word *Cotta* on them. Three minutes dragged by. Rotz was a storm building

At last a young nurse entered the room in what looked like combat fatigues. She was bright and fresh, as if fielding an order for a late breakfast.

"Four minutes," I dutifully reported, taking a seat in the lone easy chair.

Rotz roared to her, "He's DEAD, and – "

"Oh dear," the girl interrupted.

"…and this is the third time this year!"

She tried to be soothing, "He's done this three times?" she asked with some concern, while trying to find his pulse.

Rotz's mouth moved, but no words came out. While she was calling for help on her iChestThing, his eyes were darting about, looking for something that wasn't there. "Nooooo," he finally managed. "This is the third guy that's DIED in here. Can this by any chance be stopped?"

"Well, we can't be sure of anything yet, Mr. Rotzinger," she said, lamely, doing her level best to maintain a semblance of professional decorum.

But she was under assault. Rotz was exploding. "Can't you screen these guys? *Monitor* these guys? You got any idea what it's like to wake up to a dead body in your room?" He paused to catch his breath. He was at the nub of it now. "I could be *next* ya know, ever thinka that?"

This observation somehow engendered sympathy and set her to hemming and hawing.

He answered his own question. "It's fucking unpleasant."

Reinforcements arrived in the form of orderlies, and Sid and his bed were quickly unplugged from the electrical outlets and rolled out the door, bound I suppose for the emergency room. Or the morgue. The nurse glided after them, leaving a complete silence save for Rotz, who was coughing, softly. He seemed worn out.

"Did you know him?" I finally asked.

"Not really. Been in here a month or so."

"Perhaps you could ask that you not be given a roommate for a while. Tell them you think that particular corner of the room is unlucky."

"It's cursed is what it is."

"I'm sorry," I said, as sincerely as possible. I had to admit, even I was shaken by the experience. I'm not certain I'll ever forget Sid's blue face and gaping maw, as if his last act had been an attempt to call for help. It was frankly gruesome.

Rotz pointed to the empty spot where the bed and the body had so recently been. He looked at me. "That's what it always comes down to, doncha see?" he said. "That's the end, that's how it ends."

More silence.

"Marvin," it was the first time he'd used my full name, "listen carefully."

I did.

"This world can do anything it wants to you, anything you can't stop it from doing. This world will walk over you, kill your mother, destroy your children, take all your friends. Take *you*. This world doesn't give a shit." He was quieter now, sober as he stared at me. "And you gotta fight back. You gotta stand up." He waved at the pictures on the walls. "We are *Men of Cotta*," he said, "and you don't fuck with us. You wanna fuck with somebody, find somebody else. Not us."

I understood more. It was falling into some kind of a weird grouping, like a high school science project.

His voice was level now, serious, determined. "You do not put a dead person in my bedroom. You do not put me out to forage. Oh, maybe you can try, but it'll cost you. And you will lose. I will take it outta your ass. You don't come around with a bunch of chicken shit stuff and put me in some pigeon hole and feed me pablum. I go *where* I say *when* I say.

"You let this world dick with you and anything can happen. And there's no one stands up for you but you. Remember that. Cotta. You do not fuck with us."

He was finished for the day.

So was I.

But it was hardly over. I'd been blasted by intense drama twice in a single morning. I'd never seen it coming. Whatever comfort zone I'd mistakenly thought I was living in was turning out to be shaky at best, if not gone for good.

On the trip home, the question it all finally came down to was basic: What the hell was happening?

6. Names to Faces

It was beginning to occur to me that Deirdre didn't give a shit about Aunt Stephanie, had probably never given a shit about Aunt Stephanie. She'd been pretending all along – going along, getting along. It was part of her job, kind of. She had married me as a matter of course, something to be done in order to achieve the greater goal of children, children managed in a stable and reliable home environment. Deirdre was devoted to our kids, bless her heart. A great mother.

But Auntie S was not her blood, not her gene pool. Deirdre had tolerated her to keep the peace, a small price to pay for all the other stuff she wanted, the good stuff – my paychecks, the kids' soccer practices, the meaningful Halloweens, the adorable birthday parties and the rest. I could see that very clearly now – somewhere along the line I'd developed a sort of extra sense, a different, more pragmatic view of the world.

Deirdre seldom mentioned Auntie S. She would ask about her on occasion, but her mind was always elsewhere, watching her stories, cooking, straightening up, organizing stuff on her devices. After I'd tell her some made-up anecdote about Stephanie at the nursing home, Deirdre would invariably say, "That's nice," and let it go at that. I doubt she even listened to me.

I could hardly blame her. Even I hadn't spent much time looking for Aunt S at Peaceful Pastures lately. I'd always ask about her, and the reports were always positive and reassuring. However, if I didn't run into her or, more truthfully, watch her run past me, well, out of sight and out of mind. I was satisfied the staff was looking after her, and that was good enough. That's what they were paid to do.

There was always something, by contrast, to pull me back to Rotzinger. This time it was the pictures, those almost ethereal old black and white images on the walls of his room. There was also some kind of growing sense of kinship, of community or compassion. So here I was, staring out the windows of the van as it drove to Burgfort, noting the beauty of autumn leaves beginning to turn.

It was still quite warm out, which led me to hypothesize that perhaps it was not temperature that set leaves to changing color, but the angle of the sun or the shortening of the days. They were lovely, regardless of what was causing the change. They were also dying. I thought of Sid and shuddered. "Jesus Christ," I muttered to myself, which was strange, kind of. I could never recall ever muttering "Jesus Christ," or even saying it except in church, which, as luck would have it, I hadn't attended in years.

Rotzinger was waiting for me in the parlor. We exchanged pleasantries. I told him I wanted to see the photographs again. Might we go to his room? I hated to invite myself, but he didn't seem to mind.

I followed his cart down the halls and was soon standing by the wall, looking at the pictures while he sat on his bed. What most impressed me was the joy they exuded, the laughter engrafted therein. The faces were almost angelic, carefree, no self-consciousness. I mentioned this to Rotzinger and asked why.

"They were probably all drunk," he replied.

Well of course. Why hadn't I thought of that? There was no shortage of beer cans in the photos.

There were some with guys in drag, with cheap blonde costume wigs, stupid curls, enormous fake breasts, volleyballs perhaps, stuffed under T-shirts. Basically, bunches of guys having a good time. I pointed to faces and Rotz introduced me.

"Rookie, just your basic gosharooty type, the eternal kid, real straightforward, a wide receiver. He was what girls called 'cute'. That regular demeanor, the self-effacing, humble grin. He was very shy. He had marvelous hands… if a football got to them, even just to his fingertips, he held on, never dropped passes. We called him *Rook the Hook.*

And Humpy, the great sportscaster, ended up making it to the very top, the Major Leagues. Then he dies young of cancer. Man, I remember him standing on the front porch of the House talking into a rolled-up piece of paper like it was a mike, sportscasting games of tapeball we'd play in the street."

"Tapeball?"

"Yeah, you just roll up some adhesive tape until it's about the size of a softball, then play baseball with it. Can't hit it very far."

I asked about the guy giving the photographer the finger. "Hoss," Rotz said, "Housefather and fullback. Big, very strong, but agile, nimble at the same time. Look at that regular face, a central casting football face, rugged, Nordic, straightforward. Occasionally, if a game was going bad, like we were losing big, he'd insert himself into the defensive line-up without any kind of formal coach's decision, just run out there so he could hit people. He believed in physically exacting a toll on the opposition. He was angry with them for having the temerity to dare take the field against him. It was very personal with Hoss."

He laughed at a sudden, unexpected memory. "I remember one autumn, he came back to school with a foot injury, couldn't practice for a few weeks. He'd been shooting rats in a dump and had shot himself in the foot. The local paper called it a *hunting accident.*"

"Was he all there?" I asked.

"As much as any of us. Very nice guy except when he was mad, which was seldom – but then you wanted to steer clear. Then I was afraid of him. He loved to laugh though. The window curtains in his room were brassieres, a whole buncha brassieres."

"Where from?" I mumbled.

Rotz closed his eyes in thought, "Well, he had sisters and a mother, but I can't believe he'da decorated his room with their lingerie… I dunno, probably trophies of some sort. He personally led what was to be the last great panty raid at Einfahrt. The women's dorms were in three adjoining buildings shaped like a *U*. We called it *The Fertile Crescent*. At about 10 P.M. one spring night, some 200 crazed guys followed Hoss to the buildings. He stormed up to the front doors, ripped the handle off one of 'em with his bare hands, and we poured in. Many dainties were extracted before the authorities showed up and we all scattered and ran like hell. A few years later, the coed dorm concept forever ended the panty raid as an art form. All ya gotta do to get panties in college these days is open a drawer on the bureau next to yours, which takes all the fun out of it."

"Was he any kind of student?"

"Oh my, yes. Hoss read *Time Magazine* cover-to-cover every week, religiously, in an effort to broaden his mind. He was fascinated by vocabulary, by words, an avocation which, when colliding with the football helix in his head, led to incongruous epithets like *you vociferous cocksucker*."

"What happened to him?" I wondered aloud.

"Hoss's goal in life was to drive a beer truck. He wound up a postman, which is sort of the same thing. He lived in a small town with a lovely wife and kids. Great family man. At his funeral, in a little church – he died young of cancer too – his son's high school football team buddies were there. And the guy who gave the eulogy told about how before every one of their games, Hoss would give each player who requested it a list of five things to do to improve his play that day, each list personalized to that player. Very thoughtful, which was Hoss. And the eulogist asked the team, 'Guys, what was always the last item on every list?'

"They replied as one, unrehearsed, strong and loud, 'Punish 'em!' That was the essential Hoss." Rotz smiled sadly.

I pointed to a kid with a rifle. "Deadeye," Rotz said. "Used to take his .22 and shoot at squirrels in the trees out his upstairs window. Notice I said 'shoot at'. None of us could recall him ever hitting anything."

Actual gunplay in Cotta, I thought, terrific. But at least the squirrels were safe.

I asked about a short, stocky guy. "Basic Beatle," Rotz said, "loved music, loved to sing. Wore saddle shoes. Was cool. Was noisy. Would have his radio blasting early in the mornings, he'd be dancin' around.

That drove us all nuts but whattaya do – he was a morning guy. Liked the Beatles. Returned punts and kicks, very rugged but playful. Fearless. He may've been the toughest of us all, took some hellacious, high-speed wallops, just popped up and ran off the field. On freezing cold Saturday mornings before a game, he'd be boppin' around the house rubbin' his hands together in joyful anticipation saying, 'That first hit's gonna *sting.*' Became a successful college football coach, five championship teams."

"Where'd the *Basic* come from?"

"Just the word of the day, the word of the era. Like 'totally' or 'random'. He also called himself *Coleoptera,* which is the genus for beetle, or the species or something. Later, down the road, I started calling him *Guido* because he sang so much. He had great football vision, could see through all the extraneous stuff on a football field and get to the heart of the matter, then explain it in a very few words, correct the errors – saw angles and pressure points and shit. Like, when he and I were assistant coaches for the Teutons, after one game when our offense hadn't been able to run the ball, I asked him why. He replied succinctly, with that little smile of his, 'Defense stopped us.' He had uncommon clarity of insight."

I saw a picture of a huge kid with glasses and asked about him. "Dimro. Lived in the back porch room downstairs with a guy we called *Beaner.* Beaner was a wrestler, a middleweight, built like Gene Kelly, you know, the dancer? Very energetic, compact, and agile. Big Black Jack Dimro was a tackle, farm kid. Goofy. He was fond of saying 'I'm gonna bash you' to anybody who displeased him. But he was gentle about it. He became either a licensed electrician or a licensed podiatrist, I forget which. Wasn't around long. His daughter wound up going to Einfahrt. She was drop-dead gorgeous. Go figger."

And a guy who looked like a weightlifter. "Hardinger," said Rotz. "That was his real name. We called him *Hard Dinger.* We couldn't possibly have made that up, couldn't improve on it. Another wrestler. He and Bean lifted weights down in the basement. They built a little weight room, kind of. Dinger was a health nut. Then he died young while jogging. Go figger some more."

A guy with his mouth open, yelling. "That's the Hebrew. Lippy guy from New Jersey, talked like Jersey guys so naturally we called him *Hebe*. Didn't do anything much, went to classes. He was one of the guys that the Dean of Students, Obermann, put into the House without consulting us, which was his prerogative."

"What was he like?" I asked. "Geez, we had a Dean of Students where I went that was a real bear."

"Oby was a stocky guy with skinny legs. Bald, big nose, small eyes. He coached baseball too, I played for him a couple years. He knew his baseball, had played college in his youth. He was a great guy, a gentle guy. He had a sense of humor. I think, most of the time when he was dressing us down, his tongue was firmly in his cheek. He did his job and kept us on track and, frankly, it was a hopeless task because we were incorrigible. It was like trying to herd coyotes."

I had come from a gene pool that obeyed. This House was unfathomable.

"Assholes didn't last long at Einfahrt," Rotz continued, "they either reformed quickly or departed. Not sure why, but it was one good thing about the place."

"Who took all these?" I asked.

"I dunno, but Krause collected 'em. "He was one of those guys, never said much of anything, went to classes and played soccer. And then, decades later, he shows up at a funeral or something, and his daughter is a doctor with a Duke degree and he's driving the hottest BMW you've ever seen."

"Um," I said.

"Krause also used to assure us that the guilty will be rewarded and the innocent, prosecuted."

"Hard to dispute that."

"Yes, jaded before his time…"

I laughed and pointed to another face, cherubic, round cheeks.

"Bloyers," said Rotz, "another enigma. Came from the Chicago area. Completely fulla shit but an interesting guy. Very street smart. Claimed to have been adopted by a millionaire. Tried to play football but was not especially dedicated."

There were two normal-looking guys, well, except for the one wearing a fright wig. Both had strong jaws. "Linebackers," Rotz said, "great football players. Rory McRory, the guy so nice they named him twice, was an All-American. The other one, Rocky, became a head football coach, Big Ten."

"You're kidding," I said.

"Nope, and McRory turned into a famous chicken breeder, genetics and all that. And the guy with the Nazi helmet, a pulling guard, he ended up breeding pigs, lotsa pigs. He was from Port City so we called him *Port City*, or just *City*."

"Not very creative," I observed.

"Well, Port City is totally landlocked, not a hint of any large body of water within a hundred miles, and it's a real small town, that's the joke," he explained. "And then Potz, that big guy with the sideburns, the goofy grin, another wide receiver. Wide receivers are a character type, sort of. They're all lanky and loosey-goosey, and because they flank, they're apart from the mayhem in the pit, around the center of the line. So these guys were aloof, eccentric."

"Oh," I said.

"And Rug, who started selling life insurance in college and was a millionaire in his 30s. And McVeety, who could recite that *Jabberwocky* poem from *Alice in Wonderland* faster than anyone in the world – he was aristocratic, drove a cherry, white Austin Healy around, the aluminum womb. And Streaker, a quarterback – he actually streaked the campus one frigid, snowy, boring winter Saturday afternoon. Did it on a dare. Wore boots and a ski mask over his face and nothing else. Made about 15 bucks. Obermann was really pissed though, cuz that was public. Suspended him and fined him over a hundred bucks."

I noticed an enormous guy with a big smile and asked about him.

"Mouse," said Rotz.

I laughed, "Because he was so big, huh. That's funny."

"No," Rotz contradicted, "because he ate a mouse."

"Pardon me?"

"He ate a mouse," Rotz repeated.

I thought I'd misheard him. I guess I was staring in confusion. I pictured a plate, and a knife and fork.

Rotz explained. "We were in a bar one night, and we heard a mousetrap spring in the back room, and some guy brought this dead mouse out, and Mouse says, 'For ten bucks I'll eat it.' I never saw ten dollars appear on the bar faster, guys were throwing ones down with purpose. I even contributed a buck."

"Oh no," I said with disgust.

"And Mouse asked for a fresh beer. And he held the mouse up by its tail, and swallowed it whole. Never chewed or anything. He was about six feet five, weighed maybe 240. His stomach probably never even noticed it. He chased it with the beer, picked the money up from the bar, and left. It happened before most of us even realized it had happened."

"Oh god, I said, "that's unbelievably gross. I wish I'd never heard that."

"I wish I'd never seen it," Rotz allowed. "I mean, ten dollars was a lotta money back then, but it wasn't as if he had to make rent or anything. I still gag thinking about it sometimes, after all these years. I have no idea why he did it."

"No lingering illnesses or gastric disorders?"

"He obviously had great faith in the human digestive system. Although someone told me he did try to heave it up without success."

I moved to quickly change the subject, asking about a guy with kinky hair.

"Yeah, Palm Tree," said Rotz. "You got kinky black hair in Cotta, you're Palm Tree. I remember, at a Cotta Christmas gift exchange, Palm Tree had drawn Hoss's name. He gave him a bale of hay with a big red bow on it. One year he was the Cotta float in the Homecoming parade. We were playing a team with a beaver for a mascot. Now, you have a beaver mascot, you get what you deserve. Palm Tree snuck into the parade wearing a coonskin cap and a fringe jacket. He carried a rifle. He had two big signs on him, front and back, said 'Shoot the Beavers,' which back then meant 'sneak peaks at the pussies.'"

"I think it still does."

"Really?" Rotzinger's interest piqued considerably. "Great, I'm glad of that. Maybe you don't know, but we went through a period (you should pardon the expression), where the chicks were all shaving their pussies, so we kinda lost the beaver reference. I never really got that fashion statement though… gimme hair there anytime. More animal! More primal!" He smiled at me. "Encouraging that it's back." He stopped to think, lifted a palm up for emphasis. "Now, a slight *trim* I can deal with – "

I interrupted with some irritation, pulling him back to the pictures. "Who's the skinny, crazy-looking guy?" I asked, pointing to a group photo.

"Baity-ro, he came in with Palm Tree. Palm Tree golfed and Baity-ro played tennis, those non-sport sports."

Before I could speak, Rotz took the words out of my mouth, "I know, I know, not football players – but that was a lean recruiting year. Besides, we needed someone to organize the annual spring woodsy."

"What was that?" I asked.

"A sacred ritual. Every spring in May, we'd get permission from some farmer to use a spot in the country where there were trees by the River. Invite all the alums. Get a few kegs and a lotta steaks and bratwurst and grill out and just get shit-faced and puke in the woods. See that guy with the shaved head?"

I pointed to a face in the photo. It was half-sweet and half-mischievous. "Him?"

"Yeah, him, Wolfy, another wrestler. Also played football. He'd gone bald in high school, so he shaved his head. He died one of those weekends. Came back for the party on his motorcycle the night before it, Friday. Fell off in the middle of the main drag, sober as a judge, he never drank. Just a terrible accident. He was riding a cheap-ass Honda that reared up on him. Now, Harleys don't rear up, too heavy, too much bike. Did you know that?"

"How could I know that?"

"Well, I dunno. Just wondering. Have you ever driven a cycle?"

"Do bicycles count?"

"Of course not."

"I'm an avid bicyclist."

"Well, that's a start." He was only mildly annoyed. "Ever even ridden on a *motorcycle*?"

"No." I felt a bit insecure, as if my manhood had been called into question. "What difference does it make?"

"Just checking," he replied blankly with a wave of his hand, "filing it away. Anyway," he went on, "Wolfy bounced his head on the pavement, no helmet. By the time they got him to the hospital down in the city, it was too late. His parents asked that the plug be pulled on him the Sunday night after the party."

"He was at the party?"

"God no Marv, *think* before you speak. They pulled the plug after our party that he *wasn't* at. He was on life support, completely, the night of the party. When they took him off, he died immediately, couldn't make it on his own. Was a high school math teacher, maybe 23 years old, nicest guy you'd ever wanna meet. Very sad funeral, church was filled to overflowing with his students, they came in on school buses from a nearby town."

And on it went. A parade of otherwise completely unremarkable college kids but for that House thing. I was struck by a picture of two guys wearing old clothes and wide smiles, each holding an enormous, white-feathered, headless bird. One of the guys was splattered in what appeared to be blood. I was especially curious about that photo.

"Ah yes," he said, laughing. "Thanksgiving…"

7. The Great Turkey Caper

Rotzinger took a deep breath, got a wry smile on his face, and leaned back with his hands on his head, assuming the particular posture which told me a story was coming. He seemed on firm ground here.

"See, we had this tradition at Cotta," he began grandly, "we cooked a turkey dinner two days before Thanksgiving, before everyone cleared out to go home for the holiday. There were ladies in town, and coeds, they helped us with the baking and trimmings and such because our oven was small. But we provided the main course, the turkeys."

He became serious, leaned forward. "And now this was the most important element, what set our dinner apart." He paused for effect, "The turkeys had to be stolen – you couldn't just buy 'em."

"Why?"

Although I'd put him off his rhythm, he thought without rancor for a moment. "Well, buying 'em was too easy, I guess," he said. "We liked a challenge. Besides, there was an enormous turkey farm not 15 miles south of town, so it wasn't that difficult."

"Oh," I said.

"One year, Deadeye kept a live turkey up in the attic for a week, huge turkey… fed it beer to get it drunk. Man, that thing shit all over the place. I think they even butchered it up there. Whatta fuckin' mess…"

I was revolted.

Rotz didn't notice. "Now, first I gotta tell ya about Beaner, cuz this is really about him. He was this farm boy who had lived what might be called a 'sheltered' life. And his parents had told him that if he didn't smoke, drink, or swear until he was 21, they'd buy him a new car."

"That can't be true," I said, "can't be possible. Nobody does that."

"I know," Rotz allowed, "it gets no loonier. But it was true."

"Where does that happen?" I pressed him.

He was adamant. "You just hadda be there," he said. "I know, it strains credibility, but it was a fact. Beaner's favorite expletive was *jeepers creepers*. He never smoked or drank. It was, frankly, one of the squirreliest things I've ever seen."

I was certain that Rotz had seen a lot of squirrelly things, knew squirrelly well.

"Sure enough, Bean's 21st birthday came that autumn and his parents bought him a brand new, dark-green Dodge Charger. Do you know what one of *those* was?"

I pled ignorance.

"Jesus, you're hopeless," he scoffed, but he didn't say it like he meant it this time. "The Charger was only the ultimate muscle car of the era, along with the GTO. Unbelievable power, way too much power. A very sexy car. Like a mid-size sports car. Like a forerunner of the Trans Am. Sleek. Ate gas like nobody's business. And in a matter of three weeks, Beaner had two speeding tickets. If he got one more, he'd lose his license."

"I should hope," I said.

"So, well, anyway, McRory and the Buffalo were charged with stealing the turkeys that November. Nobody much planned ahead at Cotta, we were an impulsive group, and here the two of 'em were at the House and it was like 9 o'clock Monday night, and they had on gray sweat suits, and they had some kinda knife, but no chauffeur. And the only guy in the House besides them was Bean. So they asked him to drive and he immediately said no, of course, being mostly in his right mind. But Rory was a presence, and he kept after him, pressured him, and at some point Beaner relented and away they went.

"They drive to the farm, down a gravel road a good distance behind it, and Bean parks on the shoulder, turns off the engine and the lights. Buff and Rory walk across the field to the turkey pens while he waits in his new car. The idea was that they'd climb the fence, sit down motionless, grab a passing turkey, cut off its head, get another one and kill it, and leave the way they came. Since Fred was the holder and Rory the executioner, the turkeys bled on Fred.

"So while they're walking back across the field in the dark to the car, they hatch this plan. They decide to tell Bean that the farmer shot Buff. Just before they get to the road, Rory somehow gets Buff on his shoulders and carries both him and the turkeys the rest of the way. Berfel was well over 200 pounds even at that point, but Rory was a strong guy. Bean gets out of the car when he sees 'em comin' and McRory tells him that Ferd's been shot. Bean buys it. They get his lifeless body into the back seat as carefully and quickly as they can, put the dead turkeys in a gunny sack, and drop it in the trunk. Rory gets in the gunner seat and they head back to campus.

"Beaner is, of course, going the speed limit. Rory pushes him though, 'C'mon man, move this bus, I think he's dyin' back there, ya know.' Stuff like that.

"And Beaner pleads, 'I can't speed, I'll lose my license.'"

Rotz got this quizzical expression on his face, pursed his lips, and said, "I mean, ya just shake your head."

I was convulsed as he continued, "Meanwhile, Buff is layin' there tryin' not to laugh, but every once in a while he gurgles to suppress a giggle. Rory builds on that. 'See, Bean?' he says, 'dammit he's chokin' on his own blood – crank this baby into high gear.' And so on."

Rotz leaned back, put his fingertips together, and paused for effect. "One can only imagine how rapidly the tension was building in the car as Beaner was torn between losing his driver's license and having his house brother die because he didn't get him to the hospital fast enough. I mean, the deep philosophical dilemma… it must have been excruciating. Bean also, by the way, had the presence of mind to worry about Berfel bleeding on his new seats. He actually asked McRory if you could get blood offa tan leather or if it stained permanently."

Overwhelmed anew with the sheer absurdity of it all, Rotz took a second to gather himself. "As it happened, I was in the living room that night playing Pepper."

"What's that?"

"A card game, like Euchre."

"Never heard of either."

"Doesn't matter, we played for small amounts of money. Anyway, Baity-ro was there, and Wolfy, who was very good at Pepper by the way. And Black Jack Dimro was playing too. Now, we *would* let Big Jack play cards with us, but he hadda wear shoes because his feet stank so bad they made your eyes water. He had the biggest pair of wingtips I've ever seen."

I interrupted, sensing another digression. "So you were playing Pepper?"

"I'm gettin' there," Rotz assured me with a munificent wave of his hand. "And it's peaceful and quiet and alla sudden, Bean comes exploding through the front door like a madman, runnin' down the hall and into the room, literally beside himself. He's jumpin' up and down in place, waving his arms and screaming, 'Fred's been shot, Fred's been shot!' like he was crazy, which he probably was at that point.

"And sure enough, Rory drags Buff down the front hall and into the room and Buff just looked awful, covered in blood, eyes closed, laying on that ratty old gray carpet, not moving. Rory says, real matter-of-factly, 'The farmer shot him.'

"Nobody had believed Beaner, but we all believed McRory. The Baiter immediately went to the phone and was in the process of dialing an ambulance while everyone else gathered around Ferd. It was pretty heavy, all of us talking at once, arguing about what to do – like if we took him to the hospital they'd find out he'd been shot, like that woulda mattered – until Dimro called the room to order by yelling at everybody to shut up.

"When it finally got quiet, he had that goofy grin on his face and said, 'Guys, he ain't got no bullet holes in 'im.'"

Rotz blinked at me a few times. "Well, how foolish can you feel?" he finally said. "We pummeled Fred. It was a fine Thanksgiving though. Beaner was a little miffed, but he got over it. We counted our blessings. And the turkey was delicious – farm fresh, ya know?"

8. The Cotta Glee Club

I was becoming quite taken with the road to Burgfort. As September came to a close, the harvest was beginning. Enormous machines cut swaths through fields of corn and soybeans, leaving a brown and tan stubble against the black earth. Outcroppings of trees in farmyard windrows kept adding brilliant autumn colors – fire-red orange, deep burgundy, and gold – lending a bright trim to the landscape. Skies were becoming an ever crisper blue as the hot haze at last showed signs of receding for the season. Hawks perched on fence posts; geese flew in formation.

Having grown up entirely in the city, I'd never really gotten to know a country road like this one, and I found myself enjoying it immensely. I began to recognize landmarks. The rolling hills, peaceful streams and rivers, and the miles and miles of fertile fields were comforting, beautiful in their predictability and rural charm. Back home the city's freeways were choked with traffic, especially all those tiny cars that got 300 miles to a gallon of diesel. This road, by welcome contrast, was usually empty save for the occasional farm vehicle lumbering along the shoulder.

The Maple River in particular was a treasure, the perfect size, accessible and picturesque, its banks filled with thick ground vegetation and tall, venerable trees. It wound through a landscape that luxuriated under an ocean of puffy clouds, silver-white in the sunshine.

On my most recent trip to Peaceful Pastures, I had actually gotten to spend some quality time with Auntie Stephanie. I managed to catch her in her room working at her easel. It was marvelous seeing her. She looked amazing, much improved, calm and rested. She was prettier than ever, and gave me a big, warm hug and a kiss on the cheek.

She asked me how long I would be staying in Europe, when I would return. I reminded her that I was, in fact, sitting in front of her, in Iowa, talking with her at that very instant.

"Oh yes, of course," she said brightly, "silly me," and laughed. Then she suddenly sat upright with concern. "Does this mean I have to leave this wonderful hotel?" she asked.

I assured her that if she wanted to stay, it was OK with me. "Oh, I'd love to stay," she said with palpable relief, "I have so many friends here. Can I?"

Sometimes, if you just sit back and let things work out, they do.

No longer having the slightest concern in the world about Auntie S, I was free to spend my time at the nursing home with Rotzinger. It wasn't that I disliked Auntie S, not at all. On the contrary, I would always love her. But Rotzinger was coherent by contrast.

I joined him in the parlor, by the back window, asked him how he was doing.

"Not bad," he said. "They haven't put anyone in my room since Sid checked out. Much easier to get laid there now."

Not exactly what I wanted to hear, but I was getting used to such talk. What the hell, I rationalized, he'd earned it. I asked him about his daughter. He told me she'd vid now and then. She lived in California, was retired, had grandchildren. I hadn't thought to view Rotz as a great-grandfather. It put things in better perspective. Jesus. He was older than dirt. This is why he tended to wind down after about 45 minutes of conversation. He wasn't bored with me, he was simply fatigued.

I asked him how he managed to have sex so much and he told me it was the drugs, which made sense. Then he added, "Man, but the stuff they got for the ladies these days is really dynamite. Only problem is, they gotta remember to ask for it."

"They give sex drugs to you here?" I exclaimed.

"Marv, they don't pass sex drugs out, they prescribe them, *push* them. They encourage sex. They think it's healthy. It's about the only way they can get most of these people to move anymore. People here don't wanna walk around or sit on exercise bikes. But sex, that they go for."

"You're kidding."

"No," he paused to think. "Funny, isn't it," he grinned, "we had it right, way back in the Sixties – sex, drugs, and rock n roll. Now, is everyone with the program? No, you can lead a horse to water... Like, Herby, he only takes a small portion of his erectile meds. Claims he's not interested in sex, just wants to be able to pee out over his shoes."

I shook my head.

"There's always that loose screw," he said. "You think it's easy living here... one morning I'm sittin' at a table right across this room with Herby, minding my own business, we're gabbing over donuts, and man, something started smelling just awful. And I said, 'Herby, what the hell is that stink?' and Herby, he's an old German farmer ya know, he says, 'I just shit in my pants.'

"And I'm disgusted, of course, I can't believe it. I said, 'Jesus Christ Herby, go to your room and change!' And he says, 'I'm not done yet.'"

I offered sympathies as best I could. Sometimes, there are no words.

"I'm trapped in a nut farm," he sighed.

I remained focused on the appalling news of the proliferation of meds, prescribed apparently solely for recreation. "I can't believe the drugs, Rotz!" I exclaimed, "Is this even legal?"

He snapped back immediately to his game, put a fist on his open palm. "Use it or *lose* it, Marv. How'd you get to be such a prude? Some of these broads, it's the only workout they get. And this stuff they give 'em makes 'em hot to trot, let me tell you." He stared out the window.

Something was starting to dawn on me. I spoke without thinking, "Supreme?"

"Yeah?"

"Well, some of these little old ladies around here have been pinching by fanny and smiling at me when I walk by them."

"Of course, Marv," he laughed, "you're young meat."

"I'm what?" I exclaimed.

"You're fresh meat, Marv, a sex object." He was enjoying my displeasure. "They *want* you."

"That's just icky," I shivered.

"Aw c'mon," he was sympathetic, "lighten up."

I shrugged my shoulders helplessly. He turned reflective. "Why couldn't babes have been like that in college?" he mused, to no one in particular.

"Um, they got pregnant back then?" I suggested. It struck me as obvious.

"No," he said with some irritation, "they had the Pill. That wasn't it."

I had no clue.

"It was that dumb-ass double standard," he announced, "that petty morality thing. I mean, the Pill was brand new, and the mind hadn't caught up with the technology. There was a time lag."

I recalled that he was an historian. It was probably why he tended to parse things out, find explanations for behaviors in events. He studied such things.

From out of nowhere he said, "We loved to sing."

"How nice," I said.

"We had some great singers at Cotta House, and Einfahrt was known for its choirs. Ya know, Wagner, Beethoven, Bach. Music was in the German bloodline."

I was delighted that there might be at least one reference to Cotta that wasn't twisted and corrupted.

"Back then," he went on, "the Sixties ya know, toss a bottle cap over your shoulder and you hit a guitar. So we had a coupla guys played guitar, sort of. We would often sit around late at night, have a few beers and just sing."

It sounded wonderful. And while I never presumed they'd been singing *Ode to Joy* or *The Mikado*, I just sort of figured that their repertoire was confined to the pop/rock standards of the day.

"Ever hear that one about the Mexican whore?" Rotz asked earnestly.

I made the mistake of replying that I couldn't recall it, at which point he immediately gave me a spirited rendition of a verse and chorus. It was profoundly disturbing on a variety of levels, being obviously racist and sexist for openers. I furtively looked around the parlor in embarrassment. To have even been an unwitting audience to such a nauseating performance was repugnant in the extreme. The room was unaffected, however, not a head moved. I breathed a sigh of relief.

"We had a glee club," Rotz said, cheerfully noting my disfavor. "I mean, we never really had any kind of formal concert. Nobody ever paid us to sing. But we rehearsed!" The arthritic finger in the air. It was apparent that he considered this a great achievement, and I'm sure it was.

"We had parts and everything. Beatle had a strong baritone voice, was a leader in this aspect of the social agenda. And the Buffalo was a fine tenor. I know, you look at this big guy and figure he was a bass, like me, but he had a high voice, a very sweet voice. He could cover the descants on the Beach Boy stuff."

"Amazing," I observed, "you know what a descant is."

"Well, yeah," he dead-panned, "it's when you sing something and then somebody says, 'Des can't be what we wanted.'"

Although I was getting tired of having my leg pulled, I laughed my ass off. "So there was a sound track?" I asked.

"Most definitely."

"What did you listen to?"

"Well, the giants of course – Stones, Dylan, Doors, Supremes, Elvis, Temptations, Beatles, Chicago, Orbison, Credence, and so forth. And there was a carry-over from the folk scare of the early Sixties, The Kingston Trio or Peter, Paul, and Mary, stuff like that. We liked a group called *Gary Puckett and the Union Gap*, but that was probably because Puckett rhymed with fuck it."

I sighed as Rotz leapt into an enthusiastic chorus of what I assumed to be a Puckett song...

"Young girl, get outta my mind
My love for you in way outta line
Better run, girl
You're much too yooooouuuuunnnnngggggg…"

At which point, straining for a high note, his spontaneous aria disintegrated into a terrible spasm of wet coughing from deep in his lungs. He brought out a large handkerchief and began coughing into it, then wiped his face and fingers. "OK?" he said when finished, staring at me for approval.

He still looked pretty messy. "Go wash," I said.

He compliantly drove his cart over to the men's room, was gone for several minutes, and returned to pick up right where he'd left off.

"One night," he continued, "Buff announced that he had the perfect Cotta House song. And he sang it. And all the guys agreed that it was indeed *us*. I don't know where it came from. Berfel surely didn't write the damn thing. At the time it seemed as though I'd heard pieces of it somewhere before, but I couldn't place it. The melody was kind of like a march, like some Big Ten fight song, but I never could place that either. In any event, I can't imagine that whoever came up with the thing copyrighted it. It had to be public domain."

I did everything I could to prevent Rotz from singing it. Nothing worked.

"A Cotta Glee Club rendition of the song traditionally began," he explained, "with a search for the appropriate key, kind of a low drone, until everyone was in unison, on the same note. Since the first word of the song was *We're* it was a kind of *we-we-we* thing. You know, *mi mi mi*. Sort of like an orchestra tuning up."

My heart sank.

And he sang the song at the top of his lungs – lustily, robustly, jauntily – with great enthusiasm.

"We're a buncha bastards, scum of the earth
Born in a whore house, pissed on, shit on, kicked around the universe
Of all the sons-of-bitches, we are the worst
We are from Cotta House, the asshole of the earth..."

The minute he began singing I noticed a general stirring sound from the room behind me. And even as I was thinking the song could have been worse, my relief was cut short because although he was finished singing, he wasn't done. He immediately kicked into a cheer, that old 20th-century, college *siss-boom-bah* kind of thing. The clattering behind me intensified.

"Allakazoo, allakazam
Son-of-a-bitch, god damn
Shit, corruption, barrel of snot
Fifteen assholes tied in a knot
Rah, rah, lizard shit
Fuuuuuuuuuuuck"

In total it was sickening. OMG, it was awful, disgusting, worse than I'd ever imagined it could be. I was mortified. I felt permanently fouled for life for simply having heard it. I glanced over my shoulder, to the source of the sounds I'd been noticing from the outset of the rendering, a kind of metal clanging, and sure enough I watched the entire room evacuating, as if someone had yelled *Fire*. Crutches and walkers and canes and electric carts – all manner of geriatric ambulatory devices – beat a path for the exits. I guessed they'd heard the song before.

An unfortunate oldster who was out in front fell and a good part of the clacking herd stumbled over her. It looked like a train wreck in slow motion. Bodies fell on top of one another in a tangled heap. Staff was summoned to unpile them. Stern glances were shot in our direction.

I sank into my chair, trying to get smaller, less conspicuous, but Supreme went on obliviously, as if he had just shown me how some new kitchen gadget worked. "We sang it in the House," he proudly asserted, "in bars, in the caf, all over the place. People seemed to like it."

How could anybody have liked it? I wondered. But you know how it is with a song, it sticks with you whether you want it to or not, like those dumb jingles that advertise cat food and shit. On the drive back to the city, I had to keep the TV turned up to drown out that stupid melody that was churning in my head. It was catchy.

9. MITHTER EATHT THAINT LOUITH

I have no idea why it took so long for me to think of it. I guess maybe in the back of my head I had supposed I could get in trouble, or it would cause a problem. But for all Rotz's talk of beer, I'd never seen him drinking one. Based on the photographs, the elixir of choice for Cotta House was Pabst Blue Ribbon, so on my next visit I brought a few bottles of cold PBR concealed in a shoulder bag. In the past I'd carried little things for Auntie Stephanie in the same bag, and there had never been a general inspection, another advantage of a small town. In the city, I'd have been run through a full-body scanner every time I walked in the building.

I met Rotz in the parlor, told him I had beer, and asked if he would like one. He was on his way to his room before I could finish the sentence. I kept up with the cart as best I could. Once we got there, he told me to shut the door. There was no lock on it, but he said we'd be OK unless I accidentally hit a call button. He sat on his bed and I in the easy chair.

"This ain't gonna kill you is it?" I asked as I twisted the top off for him.

"They discourage me from imbibing on my own," he replied, "but all I can see that it does these days is put me to sleep. Thank god I drank a lot back when it actually got me drunk." He chuckled. "What the hell, everything in moderation. If this stuff killed, I'da been dead long ago." He lifted his bottle. "Cheers," he said, *"L'Chaim!"*

So we drank together. Rotz seemed to savor every swallow. Not that he ever needed his tongue loosened, but there is something about alcohol that engenders conviviality. "Every once in a while here, in a group meal like at Christmas, they'll give us all some beer or wine," he said, "unless somebody's chart won't allow it. You know, a little bit of red wine a day is healthy, helps keep your arteries clear. And the general mood improves with drink, more conversation." He thought a bit, then added, "And the babes loosen up too."

Rotz had a one-track mind. I asked him if he'd met Aunt Stephanie yet, and he said he had indeed. When I pressed forward, asking him if he'd made any progress, he shook his head. "She never stops running around," he said, looking somewhat helpless. "She corners a lot tighter than my cart."

Astonishing, I reflected, how life protects. I wondered if that was why Steph had never settled down with a guy and had kids, she moved too fast and too often.

I asked him about a picture on the wall of some Cotta guys with weights.

"Yeah," he said, "that's Bean and Hard Dinger. They were the weight men, along with Port. Now, Cotta wasn't really on the cutting edge of much of anything. Back then, Burgfort was this little pocket removed from the world. We were on our own track, and progress was slow. We sort of hid out from the Sixties. I mean, like I said, we caught the mood, in a way. We picked up on the personal freedom and the craziness of it, but we were spared most of that light show, the drugs and what have you."

He took a swig of beer. "Nowadays, Christ Almighty, what's that new live-through electronic stuff, you put something on your head and turn on a computer and suddenly you're in one of those fucking little boats heading for the coast of Normandy on D Day? You're barfing over the side, and the Germans are firing at you and guys are getting shot everywhere you look? What is that?"

I shrugged my shoulders.

He went on, "Or I guess you can play in a pro football game, get splattered by some 400-pound guy. And I'm sure they got X-rated sex shit on that contraption. I wonder what that's like."

As fascinating as that subject might have been, he returned directly to his original train of thought. "Back at Cotta, we had two TVs in the living room. They were those big furniture things, like wooden. On one, only the sound worked. On the other, only the picture, and it was a fuzzy black and white. You had to turn on both sets to hear and see a program. No remote control. But even if you could see stuff, actually get a picture to come in, there was nothing worth watching on it. We had about four channels, and it was all boring programs anyway."

I was literally unable to fathom such a barren video package.

"We did get NFL games on Sunday afternoons, and we'd watch those, that was right when instant replay was starting. It amazed us. And one game, they had a slo-mo iso on a pass receiver and a defender leaping up and twisting side-by-side for the ball. Baity-ro, arteest and sportscaster that he was, made this off-hand comment about how it looked like a ballet. The guys thought that was pretty ridiculous, and we laughed our butts off and never let him live it down. 'Like a ballet' slipped inexorably into the Cotta lexicon. But then, a decade later, announcers started routinely comparing such slow motion images to ballet. The Baiter had simply been prescient."

I tried to interrupt to ask him what *prescient* meant, but he was on a roll. "Baiter got married his last semester of school to some sexy wench from, well, I can't recall, some city. He moved out of Cotta and got an apartment in town with her. He invited us over to dinner one night to get acquainted and a bunch of went because it was a free meal and we wanted to check her out. So we get there and Baitman's got plenty of beer, which was good. The drinking began well, but it turned out this chick was a vegetarian. Now, back then, I think maybe I'd heard about vegetarians, but I wasn't sure they were real – I mean, I'd never met one. They were mythical creatures, like centaurs and she-males."

I suppressed a chuckle while he barreled forward. "So she had all this vegetarian food, shit I'd never seen before. Eggplant Parmesan? And that tofu stuff, which gagged me. And the centerpiece of the affair was a huge bowl of what was described as her famous *3-Bean Salad*." He stopped, put a finger to his forehead. "Gimme a sec, I can remember the beans even: limas, kidneys, and garbanzos." He sat back with satisfaction. "I remember because I'd never heard of garbanzo beans, much less tasted them. And that was the bulk of the salad, no lettuce or tomatoes. Just beans.

"Well, that salad was about the only thing on the table that any of us recognized as food, and we'd been told to bring our appetites so we were hungry. And we were trying to be polite. Long story short, we ate all the salad, finished off the beer, and got the hell outta there. About an hour later, back at the House, we all started getting a collective case of stomach cramps. The beans and beer and whatever else we ate were highly combustible, apparently. Marv, swear to god, before I knew it, my intestines were producing gas faster than I could pass it. I thought I was gonna explode. We gathered in the living room, writhing in agony, desperately ripping monstrous farts, vowing to get even with Baitman. It was Flatulence City."

I tried to find it in me to sympathize, was having trouble.

"I thought I was gonna die," he went on forcefully. "And wouldn't you know, guys started lighting 'em. Towering columns of flame shot out of their Levis; we're lucky we didn't set something on fire. We were cursing Baity-ro and his vegetarian hussy, who by the way had insisted on calling us 'Cotta boys' all night."

I laughed and shrugged my shoulders. "You lived."

"Oh god, it took forever to clear our systems. The sounds alone were riveting, not to mention the tongues of flame. Some of the guys were kneeling on the floor, asses in the air, the better to vent. It was like, well, like a ballet."

"Tell me you didn't hurt him." I was beginning to like Baity-ro.

"Nope, he moved too fast for us. He graduated and Einfahrt dealt the problem on to the world at large. I heard his divorce was quick and painful. She took him to the cleaners, got everything, his records, their beater of a car. I'm surprised he kept his wardrobe, such as it was. And although I'm sure he protested mightily, she likely wound up with custody of the recipe for the 3-bean salad. And she retained her snatch, of course, which was probably the only thing of true value up for grabs."

I was convulsed, amazed at how swiftly and completely I'd managed get comfortable with wallowing in the pervasive sexism.

"Baitman…," he said softly, "he became a long-haired hippie and…" he shook his head slowly, staring off into space. Then he suddenly snapped to and looked at me. "Where was I?" he asked.

I had to think a minute. "TV, wasn't it? The TVs? To be honest with you though, it sounded like you guys didn't really bond with TV."

"You're right," he agreed, "it wasn't central to anything. And we didn't have computers either, or video games. So what circumstance forced us to become expert at was making our own entertainment. Ours were fertile minds at work. And things were usually pretty spontaneous, like I said. And no one ever dared suggest that some hare-brained scheme was maybe a bad idea. Admonishment, curtailment, those weren't considered good form.

"And Bean and Dinger and Port were way ahead of the curve on the weight-training front, I'll give them that. There was hardly a mention of weight training in the mainstream back then. The sports gurus thought it was bad for people, like it was getting them muscle bound. It was for fairies."

"Really?" I said. "I'll be damned. I never thought about it."

"Yeah, hey, one night Port was drunk and wandered down the street to where a stop sign was banded to a telephone pole. He ripped the sign down in one pull. He was very strong. I mean, imagine that."

I had to admit it was a pretty impressive piece of senseless vandalism.

Rotz careened forward. "The guys didn't have any fancy machines, just free weights. Their corner of the basement was probably the only weight room in town. And other college guys started coming in to lift. And at some point, Dinger met a guy who worked as a baker in the supermarket across Main Street from campus. He was from Missouri, I guess. And he started coming over to lift with them. He had this unbelievable lisp, worst I ever heard. I mean, you could hardly understand him in the first place, and when he got excited, well forget about it."

I was enjoying the beer and the conversation.

Rotz asked, "Did you know that there are two *t-h* sounds in English?"

"Whattaya mean?"

"Well, there's a hard *th*, like in *the*, and a soft one, like in *thing*."

"Oh, yeah, I guess there are. What, you're a speech pathologist too?" I gently chided him.

"Well, no, but this guy, who was named Lyle as I recall, had two different lisps, a hard and a soft one. Isn't that odd?"

The range of Rotzinger's ongoing curiosities never ceased to astonish.

"He said he'd won some bodybuilding title in St. Louis, or East St. Louis come to think of it. Actually, that's across the Mississippi, in Illinois, but I suppose back then they let anyone compete since there weren't too many bodybuilders around. And Lyle was quite proud of the fact that he was *Mithter Eatht Thaint Louith*. It was his *thobriquet*, sort of. And if that weren't bad enough, central to his weight-training diet were things he called enzymes. He pronounced *enthymeth* with a hard *th* on the *zee* and then a soft one on the *ess*."

He paused to take a sip of beer. "And since lifting weights can be a lonely pursuit, and since the Cotta basement was unique in town, Lyle started coming over with increasing frequency. Beaner, especially, found the little guy entertaining at the outset, but he turned out to be a control freak which became problematic over time. Something had to be done.

"Now, Lyle subscribed to this weightlifting magazine, *Muscles and Health* or some such rag, you know, with pictures of these body builders posing, all oiled down in little thongs, the kind of thing that appeared to be pretty much gay. I don't think they even sold it in regular magazine racks back then, you bought 'em in porn shops." Rotz laughed, "But for Lyle, this periodical was the Bible. And so an elaborate connivance was concocted. I think the Buffalo was behind it, but I'm not sure.

"Anyway, it was Buffalo came to me and asked if I would help. I said sure. What Dinger and Beaner did was take a buncha pictures of themselves and the weight room. Then they wrote a letter to the muscle magazine about what they were doing and put it in an envelope with some photos. They showed it to Lyle. They never mailed the damn thing, but they assured him they had.

"See, I had just started at Einfahrt as a freshman and wasn't living in the House yet. I'd never seen Lyle, or he me. However, because I was a football recruit, I'd played the whole season and had met all the guys and they'd told me I'd be invited in soon as someone left.

"So for this deal, I was to pretend to be a reporter from the magazine, a guy who'd flown in from New York or California or wherever the fuck they published the thing to interview the lifters about their program."

"Wait a minute," I cut in. "You were only a freshman, a kid."

"Well yeah, but I had started shaving in, like, 6th grade. I had thick, black hair and tough whiskers. I had a perpetual five-o'clock shadow. I looked like I was 35. And I had a deep voice."

"Oh, OK," I said. Of course I believed him. In all the times we'd talked, he had never been wrong. There was never an inconsistency, never a mistake. His mind, at least on the subject of Cotta House, was still steel-trap.

"And so Beaner and Dinger told Lyle that this guy was coming from the magazine to interview them for an article to be run nationally. Well, Lyle went nuts. He took over all preparations because he wanted everything to be in place and accessible when I arrived. He considered himself media savvy, having come from a city.

"So the big day arrives and it's a late afternoon, classes have let out. The football season having ended, most of the guys are there when I show up. I had on a sport coat and a tie, dress penny loafers all polished and shiny. I carried a small camera which had no film in it. I did have flash cubes. I carried an attache case containing a cassette tape recorder that did have a cassette loaded. I used my own name, since Lyle and I had never seen each other. I was met at the Cotta House door by Beaner and Dinger – Lyle was laying low in the background. I was ushered immediately to the basement, introductions all around. I turned on the tape recorder. Everyone gathered to watch; there were guys from other houses and dorms as well. Lotsa people. Word had spread. It was an event."

Caught up in the sheer audacity of the scenario, I began to giggle.

"It took all of about five minutes for Lyle to take complete charge of the proceedings. The stumblebum repartee of Bean and Dinger simply didn't measure up for him. They weren't doing it right. And when I'd ask Beaner a question, he would invariably defer to Lyle – 'Jeepers creepers, I think Lyle could tell you…' stuff like that. So for the better part of an hour, Lyle waxed eloquently, lisp in full throttle, on the science of bodybuilding. It became obvious to me in but a few minutes that he hadn't the slightest idea of what the fuck he was talking about. He was completely fulla shit. For all his talk about *enthymeth*, I can't recall how it practically impacted on any sort of dietary program. I have no fucking idea where he got his *enthymeth* from."

"Maybe pills or supplements," I offered.

"Yeah, that's right, I remember now, even in the interview he was sucking on *enthyme pillth*. They were his secret weapon, how he got a leg up on the other lifters. But he never explained what they did or how they worked."

I shook my head.

Rotz barreled forward, engulfed in the memory. "I remember, when I was setting them up to take pictures, Lyle pulled off his shirt and then had to take a moment to go over into the corner and lift a few dumbbells, so he could buff his muscles out for the camera. And we're waiting for him, Dinger calling for him to get his ass over to he camera, and there was this little voice from a distant corner beyond the crowd grunting and saying stuff like, 'Jutht a thec, almotht ready.' He wasn't pumped up enough yet. I think he might have even greased his upper body down. When he returned, he struck weightlifter poses."

By this time, I was laughing so hard tears were rolling down my cheeks.

Rotz didn't crack so much as a smile, just kept telling the story. "I took a buncha pics with no film, then went on, asking probing questions while the guys watched. I was very professional, taking notes and all. I let poor Lyle wander down all sorts of crazy trails, and his spectacular inability to put anything together into any kind of coherent whole was dazzling. Every once in a while, a couple of the guys would go upstairs just to laugh their *atheth* off. I saw Hoss about ready to cry. I couldn't even glance back at him or I'da lost it. Then, upstairs they'd get the guffaws out of their system, I could hear them, and come back to the basement for more. And finally, when Lyle had run out of *thtuff* to say, I turned off the cassette recorder, thanked them all, packed my equipment in my attache, and departed.

"After Lyle left Cotta, I got a phone call in my dorm room. It was Fred, telling me to come back for the party. Oh Jesus, we couldn't stop howling. Beaner kept saying, 'I knew he'd shove us in the background and steal the spotlight.' And he sat there and beamed."

"What happened when Lyle found out there wouldn't be an article?" I managed to ask.

Rotz took a swallow of beer. "Well, I wasn't there, but he found out within a matter of days that he'd been had. And he disappeared, just disappeared. No one was ever sure quite where exactly he'd come from in the first place, or where he went. Just this eccentric spirit passing through. Such people were attracted to Cotta House like hogs to slop."

I was enjoying trying to picture the whole thing, trying to imagine how it must have been in that basement, when Rotz continued.

"Now, what you need to realize is that what we did has a name, although we didn't know it at the time. It's called *Guerilla Theater*. That is to say, you make a play out in the real world using the technique of improvisation. Sidewalk drama as it were. In this case, there were costumes involved, props, and a loose script. I mean, I had to get current on all the stuff Beaner and Dinger and Port were doing in the weight room, and I had to study weight training so I had half a grasp of what I was talking about, so I could ask reasonable questions. It had to ring true. And I did ring true."

We were both two beers to the wind at this point, and Rotz was, as promised, nodding off, worn out by his narrative. I carefully put the empty bottles and their caps back in my shoulder case, removing all evidence. He lay down peacefully on his bed to nap. I said good-bye, turned out the lights, and left.

On the drive back, I hated to admit it, but I dreaded going home to Deirdre. I preferred the company of Rotzinger and the Cotta guys. How crazy was that?

10. Feesh, Baitman, Goldy, the Jeep, and Wolfy

Octobar slowly passed. A very strong Canadian front managed to dust the pumpkins with a touch of frost, then Indian Summer arrived with temperatures in the 90s, the hottest on record. The harvest proceeded in Iowa, while in Washington D.C. clock-stoppers continued to insist, off-the-charts atmospheric carbon spikes to the contrary, that climate change wasn't happening in the first place and even if it were, America's enormous carbon footprint had nothing to do it.

This was depressing in the extreme, especially considering the fact that Japan had already entirely kicked its petroleum habit. It got solar power from satellites which converted it into electricity beamed directly to earth. My Nissan electric van purred back and forth from the city to Peaceful Pastures while I rode in air-conditioned comfort.

I would more and more get lost in thought on those trips, chewing on the shifting tides of my life. Deirdre and I didn't seem to be speaking much anymore. I wondered if Auntie Stephanie really had become more like our last child. When we moved her out, we finally had to deal with an empty nest, an adjustment leaving us nothing to talk about anymore. We'd said it all. Maybe that was it. Hell, I didn't know. What a kettle of fish. I was lost.

As my wife was fading into the background, Rotzinger was coming forward into the empty space. I wasn't sure why. He was just a slice of reality I'd never seen before, I guess. Amazingly, I would sit and listen to his stories. I could never recall just sitting with someone and listening to stories. I'd get to Burgfort, find him, and away he'd go.

This visit he began by telling me of Cletis Beasely, a hapless kid dumped into Cotta by Dean of Students Obermann, who wanted to fill a vacancy before the Cotta men could. "Oby did that to try to screw us up," Rotzinger said. "The vacancy was in Hoss's room, and we were pretty much certain Hoss would kill this new, dweeby kid. He was such a quiet little guy, squirrel bait. I think he'd flunked out of some other college. I was there the day his folks came in with him. They were short and quiet too, nice people, mousy, from some small town."

"What was Cletis like?"

"Well, he wasn't around long enough for us to really get to know him. Hoss turned out to like him and take him under his wing. He introduced him to alcohol, and even though Cletis was underage, there were plenty of guys around who were 21. Alcohol instantly became like a hobby to him. He bought all sorts of fancy drink-making stuff, martini glasses and shit, like he was in bartending school or something. He got a recipe book and experimented making different kinds of drinks. He was always quiet and off to himself. We just sorta left him alone.

"Ferd's dad had made a real nice custom bar for the Cotta basement, and we'd hired an artistic student to paint designs on the concrete brick walls down there. That's where Cletis wound up spending most of his time, drinking alone. We had neat lighting around the bar, neon beer signs and all, and one night Cletis pointed to a shadow on a wall and said it looked like a *feesh*. He meant to say *fish* but he was drunk. So we called him *Feesh* after that. A coupla weeks later he stopped attending all his classes. He was gone before the end of the semester. Dropped out. Or thrown out. Not sure which."

"What happened to him."

"Well, I'm not completely certain, but I think he became a successful superintendent of some school system in a little town somewhere."

"How?"

"I don't know. But many high school educators sprang from the Cotta ranks and many were successful." He thought for a moment, "Baity-ro, however, was not one of those."

"What's the *ro* at the end of the name for?"

"Oh, Big Jack Dimro quit football and left school, became a load-body, so we put the *ro* at the end of pretty much everybody's name, like a jab kind of."

This explained little.

"Baity-ro was the tennis player, remember? He was also a kind of thesbian type, like in plays and shit." Rotz started laughing. "You know anything about *Macbeth*?"

"Shakespeare, right?"

"Oh Marv, that's just brilliant. Yes, Shakespeare. Well, Baityman starred in an Einfahrt Players production of that play. He was Macduff. And we had this drama director who wasn't quite pulling a full wagon and who insisted on realism, so for that play he went to the local blacksmith and had a buncha big swords made."

"There was a blacksmith here?"

"Probably still is. Farmers are always breaking something made of iron or steel, discs and shit."

"Oh yeah…"

"These were heavy swords. They weren't sharp, but they were solid. They used them for props and sword fights in the play, and at the end of the last act there's this big climactic sword fight between Macbeth and Macduff. I was there for the final night of the play and they screwed up the sword fight. One of 'em slipped or something. Macbeth's sword landed smack on Macduff's forehead. Not a glancing blow either, a direct hit. It produced a sound later described to me as 'Not unlike the thud of a ball-peen hammer striking a muskmelon.' Split the Baitman's head open. Knocked him silly. He went down like a Xavier coed who just made the cheerleading squad."

"But isn't Macduff supposed to win that duel?" I asked, none too sure.

"Well, yeah, I seem to recall Macduff kills him. Fortunately, the audience was mostly made up of citizens of Burgfort and some high school kids and the few Teuton students who were there because some prof forced them to be. Nobody had a clue how it ended. I myself was deep into the REM cycle at that juncture, but my date had the presence of mind to wake me when she noticed something was happening which was perhaps out of the ordinary. I came to as Macbeth was standing over Baityman, trying to ad-lib iambic pentameter, saying shit like, 'Get thou up and take thy defeat,' and 'Ho, what ails thee villain?' and so on... It was like a ballet."

Both of us were laughing.

"And the Baitman finally comes to and stands up kinda wobbly and finishes off Macbeth and the play, and there is the curtain call and he's bleeding like a stuck pig, blood all over his face, and they hustled him to the hospital where they took about 15 stitches. He had a huge lump on his head."

He lightly scratched his forehead. "And you know, maybe that's what went wrong with the Baitguy. He was never quite right after that."

"How so?"

"He taught music in some little town and they forced him to put together a Christmas pageant and he was miffed and thought it would be funny if the elementary school kids sang 'Jiggling balls' instead of 'Jingle bells' and..." He paused. "Well, how to put this... I think Baits *underestimated the impact.* I mean, all those kindergartners singing 'jiggling balls'... small-towners tend to be conservative, straight-laced types." We were both laughing again.

"Now, that alone probably wouldna cost him his job, but he was having an illicit affair at the time with one of the matronly school board members who was married to a prominent businessman in that town."

"Oops."

"He saw this trysting as a brilliant career move, thought it was to his advantage, like she'd recommend him. One wonders precisely what she would have recommended him *for.*" Rotz paused to breathe. "I mean, there are no secrets in a small town. Things got nasty quickly. He's lucky he got out alive."

I shook my head. This was not your ordinary place, that was now completely apparent.

Rotz shrugged his shoulders. "So there went that."

"What happened?"

"I'm not real sure. Baity-ro got very far away very fast. Never heard from again."

I asked him how many Cotta men ever truly did well. I caught myself, "I mean besides you."

"Bite your tongue," he shot back, "we had wealthy guys in our ranks, lots of 'em. The Buffalo was one. He ran that boiler company he got from his dad well, was president and CEO for many decades. He married his high school sweetheart, named his only daughter Cotta, became a pillar of the community, was a member of everything: the Lions Club, Church Council, Pheasants Forever, Chamber of Commerce, the Volunteer Fire Department – "

I interrupted. "Do those things ever work?"

"What things?"

"Well, how do a bunch of guys with no training go put out a major fire?"

"I beg your pardon," he shot back. "Fred was a part of a crackerjack unit. Their motto was, 'We never lost a foundation.'"

"Um," I said.

Rotz went on. "He was a great patriarch, beloved. He had some 30 or 40 employees; they were like family. When times were lean, Ferd wouldn't take his paycheck so they could be paid. The biggest church in Montana was packed for his funeral, the flag at the fire station was at half mast. Volunteer firemen in uniform stood by their trucks and saluted as the funeral procession passed on its way to the graveyard."

"Amazing."

And Rug, hell, he was rich before he graduated. Potz became a respected educator. Course, we had swindlers too, ne'er-do-wells, but most of the boys did passing fair, whether they graduated or not."

"How many actually graduated?"

"I dunno, most I suppose. It wasn't MIT after all, it didn't take much.

Just show up and nod your head at the right times. We weren't dealing with cosmology theorists at Einfahrt." He scratched his head in thought for a second. "Maybe some *cosmetology* theorists over in the Hair and Nails Department…" he smiled. "In fact, a lot of the things that went wrong were borne by a kind of cloddish naivete, if not full-on stupidity, fueled by alcohol. Then, when the guys sobered up, they were too rattled to apply appropriate remedial steps, and things spiraled downward from there. Take Goldy and the Jeep for instance."

"OK."

"Goldy and Wolfy found a Jeep out in a field one night in the wee hours. The keys were in it, and they somehow assumed this meant it had been abandoned. So they took it."

"Whattaya mean, took it?" I asked innocently enough.

"They drove it off," he replied with a hint of disbelief himself, "drove it back to Burgfort and parked it by the House. They woke up late the next morning and realized what they'd done, a stunning clarity impressive in and of itself. But instead of returning it, they hid it. Turns out Obermann was out east with his wife on some kind of conference or sabbatical or something, and he'd left a set of keys to his house with a student charged with collecting mail and making sure all was well. Goldy pressed the kid for assistance, and the jeep wound up hidden in Oby's garage."

I don't know why I thought this was funny, but it was. "What if the Dean came back and found it?" I asked.

"Well, I don't think they thought that far ahead, lost as they were in the moment. But after a few days, the jeep came to start burning a hole in their collective consciousness. They realized that, at some juncture, the situation would become untenable. Wolfy especially was worried. So they decided, at last and to their credit, to return the thing which is, of course, what they should have done in the first place.

"Now, since they'd stolen it in the middle of the night, it made a certain sense to return it at roughly the same time, under cover of darkness. But no, they didn't drive it back at midnight but at…" he looked at me to see if I could guess.

"Noon?" I volunteered.

"Bingo," he said sharply. "And here's how you know there's a god. Goldy's driving the jeep down Main Street in Burgfort at high noon with Wolfy following in his car and, as luck would have it, the jeep's owner is sitting in the town barbershop on Main Street getting his hair cut. I would like to think that at the very moment he's telling the barber about some asshole stealing his jeep, he looks out the big picture window and sees it drive by."

"Jeez," I said.

"Yeah, the authorities were immediately contacted, an envoy was dispatched complete with sirens, and Goldy and Wolfy wound up in jail – grand theft auto."

"But they *were* returning it," I suggested in their defense.

"They hadn't returned it *yet*, it was in transit. Who knew what they were doing with it?"

"Oh, that's right. Makes sense. And...?"

"Well, like in so many similar cases, some kind of counterproductive German Lutheran forgiveness whirble kicked in, and the unfortunate and potentially embarrassing incident was swept under the rug. Fines were handed down, I believe, and Einfahrt kept both students in school paying tuition. Oby always worked closely with the authorities in town, and Burgfort understood the economic value of the College, the jobs created and monies expended on all manner of ancillary student expenses, such as food –"

"And drink," I quickly added.

"Not to mention that, which was considerable," he allowed. "And the College, knowing itself to be a small gold mine, was no stranger to twisting community arms, and 'boys will be boys,' and 'this is your last warning,' and so forth. And the whole creaking juggernaut lurched forward to another day."

As I sat back to ponder that narrative, Rotz was on to another Obermann story. "This kid who housesat for Oby told us he had a phone on a night stand by his bed," he explained, "for emergencies, I guess. The kid got the number. And Oby liked this story so much he came to tell it on himself. One night he was awakened by a call at 3 A.M. He was groggy, said hello, and the voice on the line simply asked, 'Gettin any?' and then hung up."

I have no idea why that was funny, but it was. "Do you ever run out of stories?" I asked.

"How could I?" he replied. "I mean, every day was an adventure. Stuff just happened. Like, I remember, one lazy spring Sunday afternoon, some of us are just sitting around on the front porch, enjoying the air, minding our own business, and this guy gets out of a dusty car and walks up the sidewalk to the House. Middle-aged. Dressed in a suit and tie. Turns out he's an encyclopedia salesman."

"What was he doing there, specifically?"

"Well, you'd have to ask him, but my guess was he figured that guys in college would need a set of encyclopedias."

"Really?"

"Well, back then, most every respectable home had a set of encyclopedias, it was sort of *de rigeur*. This was pre-personal computer after all, so he wasn't so far afield. The encyclopedia was the standard reference work. But, of course, he wasn't dealing with a standard buncha guys. I mean, he probably figured most of us, being students, could read. Or did read."

I was laughing again.

"And he introduces himself and comes up the steps and shakes hands all around and tells us what he's doing there, real polite-like. And he asks if anyone might be interested in buying a set of encyclopedias. And about that time Beaner comes out the front door, and we're all saying that we really would want to think about it for a while, it being a big decision and so forth, shuffling our feet. But Beaner, he quickly engages the guy, and while he allows that he personally doesn't want a set, jeepers creepers, there's a scholar upstairs who's about to graduate and who was just talking the other night about how he thinks he'll be needing a set of encyclopedias since he was going to be a school teacher, had already been hired in fact."

"Oh god." I was learning.

"And this salesmen, well he lights up like a rat in heat and hustles back to his car and brings out a big suitcase and returns to the porch and Beaner takes him in the front door and up the stairs. A couple of us followed. We couldn't believe it. Beaner though, he had this poker face, always looked innocent, if not simple. I knew him very well, and I could never tell when he was putting me on.

"So we all get upstairs and the guy Beaner was talking about was Wolfy, and Wolfy was sitting on the can takin' a shit at the time. We seldom closed that door. So there poor Wolfy was, pants around his ankles and this look of utter bewilderment on his face. And Bean introduces the salesman, and Jesus did it stink, just awful. And the guy actually opens his sample case and puts a couple encyclopedias on the fucking bathroom floor. He shakes Wolfy's hand and gives him a brochure."

I was convulsed…

"Well, we beat a hasty retreat back down the stairs, leaving the two of them to work it out."

"Did he buy anything?"

"Of course not. That sales guy musta been pretty desperate though, don'tcha think? Christ. I mean, that's insane, isn't it? I mean, isn't it? How could I make that up?"

I always tried to picture, on my way back to the city, all those marvelous characters doing all those crazy things but never was quite successful. It was an era removed. Still, it was creeping into me. I could feel it, like something I was starved for. It was human, direct. It was authentic. I once asked Rotzinger why he always talked about Cotta House and Cotta House exclusively. He would seem to have lived a full life, one with marriage and progeny involved, business and travel.

And he had pondered on that question for quite a while before he responded. "This is simply the most interesting part of my life. It has been what people have been most attracted to over the years. Oh, they'd ask about the wife and kid, they'd ask how business was, but that was just politeness. They really didn't give a damn about those answers. But Cotta is this, I dunno, this *adventure*, this departure from reality, this suspension of disbelief." He looked at me, "Think of yourself. What brings you back here? The food?"

Well of course not, it wasn't the food. Maybe it was the spirit of freedom. Maybe that was it. What an odd place to find freedom and life, I thought, Peaceful Pastures, where people were taken to die.

Cotta House

The Turkey Hunters

Party

Men of Cotta

Hoss, Mac, Rookie, and Bucky (L-R)

Wolfy and Beatle

Beaner

Rotzinger

11. POTZ AND MOONER

November brought cold, finally. And the Midwest braced itself for what was an increasingly troubling annual raft of dangerous winter storms which were tending to begin earlier in autumn and end later in spring, dumping every-increasing amounts of snow over wider areas with more ominous frequency. Winter was broadening in breadth and length. It was getting serious. Where once only cars had to be dug out, increasingly houses had to be dug out. Then there was typically massive flooding in the spring. Snow even fell copiously in Dixie.

This was no problem for the clock-stoppers, in fact they always welcomed the storms as proof that climate change was not happening. How could it have been heating up when it was snowier in the winters? Case closed. Let's go buy more petroleum and burn more coal – safer, more reliable, more time-tested. How's that new pipeline comin' along? Such ignorance was, of course, incognizant of the computer modeling begun in the 1980s and continuing uninterrupted to the present, always with the same results. When the oceans heated, inland storms increased.

As the van was driving me to Peaceful Pastures through snow flurries in early November, I got to wondering what it had been like in winter back in Rotz's day. Sure enough when I got there, he turned out to be on top of that subject as well.

"It was fucking cold," he said without hesitation. "Winter was long and snowy, maybe less so then, a bit, but it still got your attention. It was boring for us, sitting holed up by snow. We had to find things to do, invent things to do. Today, shit, kids sit on couches and goof with the latest piece of technology, vegetate their round little selves for days on end. Or they walk into some room that's a complete environment and explore that. I think my great grand kids have been on Ganymede already. Hell, why even go there for real? They tell me the view of Jupiter's Great Red Spot up close is awesome."

"I know whatcha mean," I chimed in. "No wonder kids these days are all obese, they never get any exercise. In school, instead of phys ed, they teach them how to play with computers. Makes me sick."

"We had none of that stuff, we just had our imaginations. When we got a big snow storm, we'd get bed sheets and tie 'em to a pickup like ropes and put on boots and ski through the streets of town. There was no traffic to speak of, no one but us would be dumb enough to be out in a blizzard. Of course, like as not those ventures were fueled by brandy, but what the hell, it was fun."

"The House was safe and warm, wasn't it?" I wondered.

"Not really," Rotz said with disdain. "It was colder than shit in Cotta." He paused to collect himself, "Let me backtrack to provide some context here. See, we'd come back to school every autumn and the place would look great – new furniture, walls all freshly painted, livable almost. And it would stay that way through football season, cuz the parents came in Saturdays for every home game. Mothers would bring trays of food and whatnot. And even through Thanksgiving it was nice. But about a month out from the end of football, the guys got world-weary."

"Wasn't it tedious during football season too?" I asked, "all those physical drills in practice?"

"Oh no," Rotz disagreed, "football lit us up. We got to hit people all the time, legally. And we hit tackling dummies a lot too, not to mention the ground. That gets all your aggressions out. You sleep like rocks. We were like babies during the season. We left all the bullshit on the field. We dealt with whatever problems we had violently. You were pissed

90

off at your girl? Decleat some opponent with a vicious hit. Flunking chemistry? Go flying into an opposing wedge and take out as many guys as you could."

"Makes sense," I said.

"Oh yeah, that's what football does, it calms you, empties you. Practices wore us out. All was well. We'd come home at peace. But football season would end. And in a few weeks, you'd get this growing itch to hit something, or somebody, so you threw a shoulder into some house brother in the living room and he fell against a door. Maybe he weighed over 200 pounds. Well, the door broke, shattered. Or two big guys had a wrestling match in the living room. Boom, there went the coffee table. Some guy lands on it and it's wood scraps."

He was so matter-of-fact about this, it was nutty. I struggled to even envision it. For him, it was the way things had been, so it made sense.

"And then, say you're cranky and drinking a beer in what was left of the living room and, well, for no reason, you throw a half-filled can at a wall. Maybe you're pissed, maybe you're just fucked up. But you throw it. And it hits the wall and knocks off some plaster. Well, that's a start. And then other guys do it. And Hoss especially had a penchant for putting a fist or an elbow through a wall when he got pissed. Which means by the time spring rolls around, there's barely an inner wall there, just a bunch of big holes. And slats of wood.

"And we discovered, quite by accident and to our perfect amazement, staring into the holes in the wall one night, that there was really no insulation to speak of in the place. It was an old house. This explained much, actually, as regarded winter. Coupled with pre-Coolidge wooden window frames and single-pane glass, we came to realize why when the wind blew outside, it seemed to be blowing *inside* as well. There was always this hefty, conspicuous draft. And then the ancient furnace was operating at maybe 10% capacity. So it was just plain chilly.

"We had a running back, short stocky little guy with narrow eyes, so we called him *Suzuki*, naturally."

I interrupted. "You guys were racist and sexist. Do you realize that?'

91

Rotz took exception. "We weren't racist. We didn't think we were better than Asian guys or black guys, we just noticed they looked different and acted different. However, on the chick thing, you have a valid point. Chicks were whacked then, but hey, they're whacked today. I'm not sure how they keep getting away with it." He looked down for a minute. "Oh yeah," he returned his gaze and continued, "that's right, I remember now, they make the babies."

He shook his head as if to clear it and picked up right where he'd left off. "Zuki had a small, portable, electric space heater. Guys went wherever he went in the House, followed him around because it was warm where he was."

"Couldn't you complain to the College?" I wondered aloud, and knew the answer the minute I'd said it.

"No," Rotz replied, "in the first place they didn't give a shit, and what were they gonna do anyway? But in a larger sense, we loved the House and didn't want company. We didn't want to owe Obermann anything. We kept to ourselves. We bundled up. Sometimes you could see your breath in the living room. It became part of the charm of the place."

The more I discovered of the nature of Cotta House, the more I realized that it was the living embodiment of Murphy's Law. Whatever could possibly go wrong had kept going wrong, all the time, over and over.

"One winter's night, midweek, it was cold. The wind was blowing. It was January, I think. It was snowing heavily. Some guys were in the back of the living room playing Pepper at the card table."

"It was still standing?" I asked.

"Oh hell yes, the card table was sacred, what with Pepper being played there for pocket change. No one dared wreck that."

"Oh, OK," I said, "just checking."

"Anyway, Potz and I lived upstairs next to the bathroom. And in our room, by the window, was this metal box bolted to the floor and containing a chain-link ladder."

"What?" I said without realizing it.

"A primitive fire escape," Rotz said. "The town fire department probably forced them to put it there to quasi-comply with fire codes, some cosmetic bullshit, a stab at relevance. In the event of fire, you lifted back the top of the box, opened the window, tossed the ladder out, and climbed down."

"No smoke alarms?" I asked.

"Not for another few decades," he sighed. "Well, Potz was bored. He was an All-Conference wide receiver who played with little regard for his body, and he'd separated his shoulder at the end of the season. So he'd had recent surgery, which meant he was walking around with his right arm in a sling. And, as I remember, we were drinking. 'Tell you what,' he says to me, 'I'll take all my clothes off and climb down on that fire ladder.'"

Rotz paused as his fingers tapped the side of his forehead. I wondered aloud what would be the point of that.

He went on, patiently explaining, "I asked him the same question. Potz had apparently thought this through a bit, and he'd calculated that the ladder would come down on the outside of the big set of windows at the back of the living room, where the guys were playing cards. I would go down and stand by the card players. Potz would descend on the ladder, get into mooning position, at which time I would say to the guys, 'Hey, look out there,' and they'd look up to see Potz's bare ass staring back at them."

I asked why this would have any entertainment value in the least.

Rotzinger thought for a bit. Then he put his palms up helplessly. "I don't know," he finally said. "Even to me it sounded like a bad idea at the time. But, it was there to be done. And, sure enough, Potz undresses and carefully lets the ladder down outside the House, so as not to make any noise. He climbs out the window, into the blizzard and onto the ladder, one arm in a sling mind you, buck naked, and begins to gingerly lower himself.

"Well, I casually stroll downstairs as instructed, take up a position leaning against the wall opposite the window, and watch Potz laboriously descending, completely unnoticed by the Pepper players. I could see his feet first, ghostlike in the snowflakes, then his legs, then his privates. And sure enough, hanging on the ladder with one arm, he turns and bends over with his backside to the window. It was surreal, this shadowy, white, naked guy out in the dark through the window in a snow storm."

Rotz scratched the top of his bald head if he were trying to remember something even he couldn't believe.

"God works in mysterious ways," he finally continued, "and just as I'm telling the guys to look out the window, and just as they're lazily glancing up, a powerful gust of wind pushes Potz and the ladder well away from the House, then suddenly quits, and he swings inexorably back, still bent over, bless his heart. His bare ass hits the window first, coming into the room with a great crash, smashing all the glass and the window frames and everything. Splinters of glass are flying everywhere. He did somehow keep his hold on the ladder, until it swung back outside and he let go and fell into the snow. And, you know, the guys were so calloused to that kinda shit, I can't remember them jumping up or in any way showing any kind of surprise. They just went back to their cards. One of them might have told Potz to fix the fuckin' window, but that was it."

I was laughing so hard I could barely speak. "Did anybody get hurt?"

"Miraculously, no. Oh maybe Potz got a little cut or two on his butt. But nothing. The storm, however, was now literally *in* the dining area, snow flurries blowing around. I think we managed to find some big piece of plywood to nail up to get us through the night. The guys moved their game to the basement. And we did have to report that incident to the powers that were, as we needed the windows replaced."

I shook my head. I tried to piece things together. "Excuse me," I asked, "but I can't remember, is this Potz fellow the guy who went on to become a successful high school person?"

"Award-winning," Rotz confirmed. "Outstanding administrator and family man."

"Great Christ," I said.

"Also the valedictorian of his high school class."

"So he was smart?"

"Ostensibly."

"What," I sniffed, "class of five?"

"Noooo," Rotz evenly corrected me, "probably about 40 or 50, average for an Iowa small town at the time."

"Still, small," I argued. "But a lotta Cotta men wound up working with impressionable young minds."

"Interesting, isn't it," he replied.

"More like disquieting," I said.

"Yeah but think about it," he countered, "we'd been to the edge of the chasm, had stared down into the abyss. Who better to teach kids how to do things right?"

As usual, I was forced to concede that he had a point. I returned him to the mooning.

"I'm not sure what explained the spate of mooning back then," he continued. "Dinger was an inveterate mooner. What with all the weight-lifting, he had a pretty solid body and accompanying ass. Girls always seemed to be cruising by the House in cars, and he would on occasion moon them out the front bedroom window. One afternoon, while he was raising the shade, something got stuck and the whole contraption, curtains and all, fell on him and he got tangled up in it. He was standing there in his birthday suit trying to extricate himself. Then he tripped and fell over. There went his anonymity, not to mention dignity.

"And one night shortly before a Christmas break, instead of putting up a tree, six of us formed a human moon pyramid in front of the picture window in the living room, then opened the drapes. We heard roars of approval from the street, horns honking and what have you, and I'm told the effect was dazzling. I never saw it, of course, since I was in the middle of the bottom row – no pun intended."

"Wasn't that against the law?" I asked.

"Well, yes, now that you mention it, it was," he replied. "Matter of fact, we had a guy in Cotta we actually called *Mooner* who ran afoul of the law. For him, mooning was a way of life. There was a big school nearby, a university, about 20 miles south in Maple Falls. Mooner was in the backseat of a car with a couple of guys one winter night, cruising through that campus, indiscriminately mooning anyone he could find who was out and about, which I guess was fun for him. Until he was arrested. Caught in the act, red-handed so to speak.

"Well, he could have accepted the sentence, which was a stiff fine, or he could go down to Maple Falls and argue his case, which he decided to do. And he winds up one spring afternoon, prepared as best he could be to defend himself, in a court room."

"Why not get a lawyer?" I suggested.

"Well, they cost money, and it was kind of small potatoes, and I think Mooner failed to grasp what the trial itself would entail. I'm not sure he realized he'd be in a courtroom filled with a surfeit of defendants waiting to plead their separate cases. I think maybe he thought he might be alone."

"But he wasn't," I said.

"No, he wasn't," Rotz said in a resigned tone, "there were maybe 30 people packed in there. So now Mooner doesn't quite know what to do. And as luck would have it, his name was one of the first to be called, and he walks to the front of the courtroom where the arresting officer is waiting to argue the people's case. The official complaint was *indecent exposure*, and it turned out the judge wanted to know what that might have meant, in practical terms. What with the unanticipated formality of it all, complete with a judge in robe, a bailiff, and a court recorder who administered the oath, somewhere along the line Mooner had decided to simply plead guilty, pay the fine, let it go at that, and get the hell outta there. But he hadn't anticipated the judge's curiosity either.

"Now the judge was an old man, and he looks down at Mooner from the bench, (and Mooner had the face of a choirboy), and the judge says, 'Indecent exposure?' as if he can't quite believe it. Mooner just pleads guilty again, but the judge won't be sidetracked so easily. 'What do you mean by *indecent exposure*,' he asked aloud, somewhat bewildered. When Mooner hemmed and hawed, the arresting officer, who was indignant, was quick to assist. 'Your honor, this is that mooning incident on University Hill,' he stated authoritatively and with some malice.

"The judge was non-plussed, confused. He said, to no one in particular, '*Mooning*, what's mooning?'

"At this point, Mooner was simply looking for any way out, any exit route would have sufficed. He later told me he wished a hole would have appeared in the floor that he could have dropped through. He was tongue-tied, embarrassed, trapped. He would speak of whispered laughter rippling through the assembled throng, of feeling his face getting hot.

"Once again," Rotz narrated with a completely straight face, "the arresting officer came to the judge's assistance. In a firm, loud voice he announced, 'Mooning is hangin' your bare butt out a car window, your honor.' Well, the courtroom came unglued, as you might expect."

Rotz waited patiently while I tried to stop laughing. When I'd regained some composure, he went on. "And the judge peered down at Mooner, paused while he thought, and then simply asked incredulously, 'Why? *Why?*'"

"My question exactly," I said, laughing.

Rotz didn't even try to explain, just barreled forward. "Mooner was a feisty little guy. There was the time a bunch of us drove in caravan to Lower Iowa University for a basketball game, drinking all the way. And we were sitting in the stands near a buncha black guys who were rooting for the home team. We were cheering for our Teutons, naturally, and Mooner was always a very vocal athletic supporter.

"And at one point, one of the black guys is offended and screams at Mooner, 'Shut up mutherfucker!' And Mooner shoots back, 'Well, if you'd get your fuckin' mother off the streets, maybe I wouldn't be fuckin' her.' That's when the fight started. It was a big one, a brawl really. They had to stop the game for a while. We were escorted out of the gym and ushered to our cars and shown to the edge of town and strongly encouraged to take the blacktop back to Burgfort."

"Was Mooner by any chance a football player?" I asked.

"Defensive back," Rotz confirmed.

As the car drove me home, I realized I was getting curious about football of all things…

12. Football

A week later I was making my next trip to Peaceful Pastures. The football season was in full swing. I'd never paid much attention to the sport but having listened to Rotzinger talk about it so much, I'd started to watch 3D podcasts and even attended some local high school games in an attempt to figure the thing out. I listened to the commentators and tried to understand the rules. Turned out they were pretty simple, really, just take over enemy territory with ruthless might and heartless guile, as Rotz had accurately described it.

When I got to the parlor, he greeted me and quickly led me to his room. I opened the beers and asked if he'd like to talk about football. He was more than up to the task.

"Look," I began, "I'm watching these guys out in the middle of August, practicing in all this bulky padding, helmets and whatnot when it's 100 degrees and humid. I mean, kids are dying around the country at football practices, not from the contact but just from the heat. Then, I've seen the pros play in sub-zero temperatures in blizzards in January. Rotz, I got just one question…"

"Shoot," he said.

"That judge's question… Why?"

He thought for a long time, sipping his beer. Finally, he said, "Nobody's ever really asked me that before." He seemed puzzled.

I tried to help. "I mean, was it for the glory?"

"There was seldom any glory," he replied. "Girls maybe but not glory. And girls were pretty important back then."

"Did you wanna turn pro? Make a fortune?"

"No, that never really occurred to me, although there were guys from our conference who made it in the pros and did very well. I never wanted to play football for a living."

I was back to square one. "Then *why?*" It was bothering me. "Why are all these people playing football. It looks so dangerous."

"Well, that it is," said Rotz, as he took a swallow of beer and belched loudly. "Damn, that felt good," he said without apology. "I hated football practices but loved the games. It was all about the games. It was just so much fun."

He saw that I wasn't really getting it. "Look," he explained, "it's adrenalin. It's that rush of adrenalin. Football is combat, pure and simple. And it unleashes a huge rush of adrenalin, and you get to hit guys hard, over and over, and get hit. And because of the adrenalin, you don't feel it, until the next day that is. Now, for me it was always better to hit than be hit. But either way, it was good.

"That guy on the other side of the line… last play he slipped your block. This play, the sunovabitch wasn't gonna slip your block. You were gonna put him on his ass. That's how you think. It's therapeutic. Watch kids play, little boys. They chase each other around and catch each other and fall down and pile on. I'm not sure why that's so satisfying, but it is. Long as there are little boys who want to be men, there will be football. Didn't you ever run around jumping on guys in piles on a playground?"

I thought a bit. "I can't recall."

"Well, now, apologies for intruding," Rotz said gently, "but were you ever allowed to grow up?"

"Whattaya mean?" I shot back.

"Heyyyy, no offense," Rotz was calm, "and I don't wanna spill beans here, but Steph has talked about her big sister…"

"She has? You know Aunt Stephanie that well?"

"Marv, there ain't that much to do around here. I've made some progress. Yeah, we talk."

"She remembers Mom?"

"Of course she does. Says your mom was a bit overbearing, always bossing her around, always the goody-two-shoes type. Drove Steph crazy. Of course Steph liked her, but she was under your mom's thumb for a good part of her life."

I was thunderstruck. How could poor, addled old Auntie Stephanie have managed to communicate all that? "So, you're friends?" I asked.

"I guess," he replied. "Hey, she's cool, she's fun, she's beautiful, and whatta setta jugs –"

"Aw, c'mon Rotz," I pleaded. "It's my Auntie S, and –"

"OK," he said, smiling. "OK. But I'd be willing to bet that your sainted momma was pretty domineering with you too."

I stopped to think. Well, yes, she had been. I had to admit.

Rotz continued, "You went straight from your mom to your wife, who, Steph says, is also domineering."

I instinctively leapt to Deirdre's defense, but my heart wasn't in it. He had me cold. That was it, pretty much exactly. I was suddenly demoralized and distracted. It was a bobcat dropped in my lap. I'd have to do a lotta thinking about it.

"Can we get back to football?" I weakly asked.

"Sure," he said. "Where were we?"

"I dunno," I allowed, "anywhere."

"OK. Have I mentioned our coach?"

"No."

"OK, well, we had a great coach, Lou Banstra, a guy who'd played for Lombardi in the NFL –"

"They had an NFL team in *Italy* back then?" I exclaimed.

He gave me one of his deprecating looks that told me he thought I'd said something dumb again. He addressed me as if I were a five-year-old, slowly and carefully. "No, the NFL coach was Vince Lombardi, of the Green Bay Packers. Banstra played offensive tackle for him. Lombardi won the first two Super Bowls."

"Oh," I said, duly chastised.

Rotz ignored me and continued. "Lombardi was a big nut about physical conditioning. And I guarantee you, whatever drills the Packers did under Lombardi, we did more reps of them under Banstra. He worked us unmercifully. But it paid off, we won a championship. Now, ya gotta understand, Einfahrt had done nothing but lose football games for a long time. I think the team had won four times in the past three years, Banstra's first three years of coaching. The seniors, like Rookie, had done all that work for only four wins. The previous year, my freshman year, we won one. Humpy had a pregame interview show he taped with the coach called *Banstra Before Battle*. Midway through that season he was thinking of changing it to *Lou Before Losing*."

I laughed. Supreme didn't.

"It wasn't funny, and it wasn't fun. We didn't believe in him, and we didn't believe in ourselves. Losing, like winning, is contagious. Hard to recruit good talent when you're losing.

"But we got lucky that season. The fates smiled on us. Estimable players just fell into our laps. Like, a new Dean of the Faculty came in from the East Coast and brought his son, a kid named Conrad. We called him Connie. He was a linebacker, big and fast and strong. Man, could he hit. And we got Rory McRory too, another linebacker, from a junior college. Those two guys were amazing, worked together like twins.

And there was Rocky, also a linebacker. He was from a Catholic school of all things. He lived in Indiana, was conned into visiting Einfahrt by Bloyers, who'd graduated and gotten a job as an Einfahrt Admissions Counselor. He was on a recruiting trip and bullshat Rocky into thinking he was a coach. So Rocky and his high school coach show up in Burgfort that summer and walk into the Athletic offices and run into Banstra and ask where Coach Bloyers was. And Banstra says, with some indignation, 'Coach who?' Oh god…"

I was laughing again.

"But in spite of Bloyers, or maybe because of him, Rocky came to Einfahrt. And brought some classmates who played too, Mooner and Streaker and a few others. I mean, it was an amazing season. Injured guys came back healthy. We got a coupla black speed merchants outta Waterloo and Racine. It was like the planets lined up."

He stopped to breathe, and to remember. "What a buncha guys." He looked up to the old black and white team picture on the wall, the one that said *Champions* on it. "I can tell you every one of their names," he said, and there must've been 60 guys in the photo.

"Banstra worked us within an inch of our lives," he went on. "We did grass drills until hell wouldn't have it. Grass drills. You run in place, knees high, until the coach blows his whistle. Then you fall on the grass on your stomach. When he blows his whistle, you're up and running in place again. There was a baseball diamond on our practice fields. Banstra liked to have us run grass drills on it because to fall on the dirt was harder and grittier, more unpleasant.

"I remember one afternoon, I was doing grass drills next to Connie, and whenever we'd hit the ground there was this odd thumping noise coming from him. Between whistles I managed to ask him what it was, and he said he was hitting the ground head-first in hopes he'd knock himself out because he couldn't stand the pain."

"That's nuts," I interrupted.

"Yeah, well, that's football. It's like, 'Are you man enough to get through it?' It was this primal kind of survival thing, a gauntlet to be run, a pubic rite. Guys would quit the team. They couldn't stand the practices. The pansies were cut from the herd. Really good football players walked away."

I was beginning to comprehend, a little.

"One afternoon, we were practicing offensive plays, and Port City, who was a pulling guard, jumped the snap count, moved before the center snapped the ball. Banstra was upset and yells at us, cuz it was a simple mental error. There wasn't even a defense in front of us. So we line up and Port jumps early again. Now Banstra's pissed, and he threatens retribution if it happens again. Well, Rory was in working with the offense that day, playing the other guard spot, and he's a co-captain, and we get back to the huddle and *he* gives us hell. 'I don't wanna be runnin laps you assholes,' he says, 'so fucking get it right.' So we go back to the line and *he* jumps. Banstra hits the ceiling, and we're runnin' laps around the field. Now, Potz, being a wide receiver, is in on every other play, and he hadn't even been on the field with that group, but he has to run laps too, and he's goin, 'What the fuck am I doing runnin' laps, I wasn't even *in* there.' We musta run 15 minutes."

"No justice," I laughed.

"And no mercy," said Rotz with a smile. "But Banstra said we'd never lose a fourth quarter and we never did. We were in shape. And, you know, just being in great shape was exhilarating. Each of us was physically powerful, as powerful as he could get. As powerful as we would ever be. The fullness of youth. All sorts of life lessons there."

He closed his eyes and went on, "And then there's autumn itself, just autumn, those perfect days, football weather, brisk air and hot sun. I can still feel the warmth of the sun on my uniform, Marv, on my arms and face. You just wanna go out and run and hit people on those kind of days…"

A soft knock on the door brought us from the playing fields back to the room. I immediately hustled to grab the empty beer bottles and hide them in my bag like, well, like a school boy. "Enterrrrrr!!" Rotz roared, as best he could roar. Aunt Stephanie burst into the room, confirming my worst fears. She was surprised to see me. I was surprised she remembered me.

"Marvin," she said, "what are *you* doing here?"

"Looking for you," I lied, "but I can never find you. So I talk to Rotz."

"Oh," she said, "well, I'm very busy here." In the background, Rotz chortled, causing Auntie to actually get flustered. "Er, how have you been?" she asked.

"Oh, fine," I replied, "we miss you."

"I'm happy here," she said.

"Great," I said. "I'm so glad." That was the truth.

"Hey Marvin?" Stephanie asked, "I need a favor."

"Sure," I replied, "what can I do?"

" I wanna invite Supreme home for Thanksgiving."

I said fine. I was surprised she even remembered Thanksgiving, much less wanted to join us for it with Rotz. I was delighted; so was she. She gave me the biggest, longest hug.

When I got back to the city, though, Deirdre amazed me, going ballistic at the thought of sweet Auntie Stephanie even coming to visit for Thanksgiving in the first place, much less the prospect of entertaining another old person besides her. I told Dee she could invite her family if she liked, make it a big gathering, but she didn't want to entertain period. I told her I'd take care of the preparations, we could even have the event catered. I told her I thought it the right thing to do.

"Who's this Supreme guy?" she stormed. "He sounds like some kinda nut."

"I dunno," I lied, "one of her friends at Peaceful Pastures, I guess."

"What's he like?"

"I don't know," I said, more firmly. "How'm I supposed to know? Don't you think it's nice that Stephanie has found friends at that place?"

Her response stunned me. It was patronizing, she talked to me like I was a schoolboy – I could see that clearly now. "Marvin, listen carefully, Auntie Stephanie is lost to us. She's lost to herself. She'll never be Auntie S again. She's just heading for oblivion. I'm sorry, but she might not even remember us if she would get here to visit. I know it's hard, Marv, but that's reality. You gotta let her go."

"But she's still *there*, Deirdre," I said as kindly as possible, ignoring her insulting tone, "in fact, she's more there these days than when we put her in that place."

My wife went back on the attack, "Mary-Mother-of-God, Marv, how're we gonna take care of this Supreme guy? Does he wear diapers? I ain't dealin' with an old fart in diapers. Is he gonna die on us? Does he have to spend the night? Does he even have a name?"

Now I was indignant. "Yeah, he has a name. It's Rotzinger. And yes, he spends the night with us, I'm not makin' two trips to Iowa the same day. I don't think he's in diapers. He can't walk very well, but he's a nice guy. This is my house too, and I already told Steph she could bring him. I'm sorry…"

"How *could you*? Without asking *me*?"

"What was I supposed to say when she asked, Dee? Fuck, she's my kin."

"Watch your language!" came the loud retort. God, Deirdre could be such a schtup sometimes, what with her tight-assed rules crap. She could not be placated. "Judas Priest Marv, I give up, you do the entertaining. You can get the food. You can serve and clean up. Come to think of it, you can have the house the whole damn weekend if you want. I'll go to my brother's place." He lived three hours to the south.

And that was that.

The trio of us vagabonds would celebrate Thanksgiving together, and Rotz would stay the weekend at my place with Steph. It was almost a relief that Deirdre wouldn't be there; we wouldn't have to deal with her. Steph and Supreme could even sleep in the same bed if they wanted.

13. THOSE WHO STAY

There was a nice, gracious joy in the van the night before Thanksgiving as it drove the three of us home on that quaint, winding country road I'd grown to love so much, through a dusting of snow flurries that danced in the headlights. Rotz's little electric cart was in the cargo space, and Steph was in the back seats, burbling. Classical music gently played on the surround system. Rotz was in front with me, lounging and sipping a beer, talking football.

"Our first game that championship season was non-conference," he began. "We were picked to lose, of course. Losing is what we did. But we didn't lose, we won – seven-zip. Coach Banstra said it was the first time he'd ever been undefeated."

"How many games did you lose that season?"

"None in the regular season. We tied the next game, the first conference game, against the favorite to win the title that year. Then we ran the table. There was that one tie, but the rest were wins. We played every team in the Conference and beat 'em, soundly mostly. All the old nemeses. I think we snuck up on some, they just couldn't believe we'd gotten so good so quick, until we ran over them. It was sweet, it was."

"But how?" I wondered aloud.

"Well, we started believing early, only a couple of games in. Just *felt* different. The guys made a pact before the season started that we wouldn't drink any beer until the season ended –"

"This was a big deal?" I ventured.

Rotz thought for a minute. "One summer, the College maintenance guys came into Cotta to try to paste it back together for yet another school year. And the place was its usual disaster area. It stank of stale cigarette smoke and stale beer and stale god-knows-what that we hadn't cleaned up. Of course, come to think of it, we never cleaned up, which was part of the problem.

"Couldn't you hire a cleaning person?"

"First of all, that cost money. Second, we kinda liked it the way it was. Anyway, these guys were poking around down in the basement, in the room where the furnace was, and there was this false wall, open at the top, went the entire length of the room. So they ripped it out and found it was filled floor to ceiling with empty beer cans and bottles. Hundreds of them, if not thousands. The place did smell better that next year."

I shook my head, smiling. These guys were total animals.

"That wasn't the only major sacrifice, the beer celibacy," Rotz continued. "We did whatever it took to make the team work. Like, Hoss was a fine runner, a fullback, could catch passes too. But the coaches had him mostly blocking for Bucky, the tailback, and he accepted that role. Few running backs would.

"And Rookie, who was the other co-captain and a senior, was only a couple of catches shy of the school record for career receptions after his junior year. They switched him to defensive corner, because he had experience, and defense requires more decision-making than offense. He was great on D. Instead of quitting like some prima donna, he went out and played with complete commitment and was named All-Conference. He didn't care about a personal record; he became a champion. We hadda buncha guys make All-Conference, including me, and our entire backfield."

"Congratulations," I said.

"Over half of us were from Cotta. Rory was MVP of the Conference and the team. He played both ways all year."

"Both ways?"

"Guard on offense – linebacker on defense. Very difficult to do. See

Marv, we weren't fancy. Everyone knew what we were going to do. We were either going to hand the ball to Bucky, or Speckle would pass the thing. But we executed very well. It was really about execution. They couldn't stop us.

"Our defensive coach, Jetson, kept telling us to play with 'reckless abandon', and that's what we did. I can still hear him screaming at me. 'I could eat a pound of hamburger and *shit* a better football player than you!' Oh my..." Rotz smiled and plowed forward, totally caught up in the memories, "That season, we had speed."

"So you didn't drink, but you did do performance-enhancing drugs?"

"No Marv, you putz, *speed*, we were *fast*. We could run like the wind. All the backs and receivers had to run a half mile in 2 minutes 25 seconds. Linemen in 2½ minutes."

"Sounds hard," I said.

"Try it some time. So the third game we just blasted this team, shut 'em out, scored like 40. Which meant that in three games, our offense had scored more points than the entire previous season."

"Any close games, like dramatic?" I asked.

"Nope," he replied simply. "We just started setting records. Bucky ran for over 300 yards in one game, a blowout. Course, Hoss was in front of him clearing the way every play, opening holes. And Speckle, the QB, oh my did he have a season. He had come from a Big 10 school a couple years earlier. He threw a wonderful ball, tight spiral, landed soft. Very accurate. Just a great passer. He was a fine singer too, a tenor."

"So 300 yards is a lot?"

"Three football fields, Marv. In college ball, that's damn near impossible. Never happens in the pros."

"Undefeated, nice going Supreme," I said with genuine respect.

"Well, not quite. We went to the playoffs then. And we lost our first playoff game to a team from the other side of the State. Lost by a touchdown."

"I'm sorry," I commiserated.

"Yeah, well, we couldn't see the playoffs. We were focused on winning the conference, something Einfahrt hadn't done in a decade. That was about as far as our heads could go. We went from last to first, and that took all our mental toughness, that achievement. But it turned things around for the Teutons. They went on to build an enormous winning tradition. For the teams that followed us, winning the conference was a given. They could point to the playoffs, and that enabled them to start winning playoff games regularly. And the basketball players were winning conference championships back then, and the wrestlers started to win big too. The entire school changed."

Rotz stopped talking and was fiddling around under a dash light, trying to get his wallet out. While he was quiet, I imagined what it must have been like. What those guys did. They lived in squalor and loved it. They were complete losers. They must have had every reason to phone in a season or simply quit. Instead, they had stepped up and achieved. Quite something...

"Found it," Rotz exclaimed, and held up to the light a small card he'd fished from his worn old leather wallet. He read solemnly. "Quitting comes easy for many people. Many do not want to pay the price to be a winner. It requires little effort to be a loser, and anyone who chooses that path can succeed at it. But those who stay will be champions and will become winners not only on the football field but in life itself. As for those who drop out because the going gets too tough, who knows what happens to them."

"Nice," I said.

"That was Banstra," he said with reverence. "He died of a cancer he fought for years – Rookie, Beatle, Rory, and I went to his funeral. Just had to pay our respects. It was very sad. But we were grateful for the impact he'd had on our lives."

Silence...

"I was a cheerleader," Auntie Steph chirped from the back seat. "I loved to watch football. Those sidelines, it was like a war, a battle, very military. Stimulating too, all those hormones. Supreme is a dream come true. My football hero."

I was stupefied. Where had her encroaching dementia gone?

"So the season ended," Rotz was on a new jag, "and naturally we had to celebrate. Pretty much the entire team goes to this little bar in a small, nearby town to drink heavily, and as you might suppose, the majority of the team was underage. But this joint didn't card, and the owner saw all this business coming and, well, away it went. Shit, that first beer tasted awfully good, as did the next six or seven. And, wouldn't you know, the thing got completely out of hand and there was a lotta traffic and cars and noise, what with all the bodies, and some douche alerted the law enforcement guys and…"

His voice trailed off, there was a distant look in his eyes, and he smiled. "Oby, being on excellent terms with all the law guys around there, got a call from somebody with the cops who tipped him off, told him that if he could get all the Einfahrters outta there, then the police wouldn't come crashing in and arrest everybody."

"How many people were there?"

"I dunno. There was a lotta coming and going, guys outside. I'll say 50 to 100. Girls too of course. In total, a sizable percentage of the Einfahrt student body, let's say that."

I laughed.

"So Oby drives down there personally and storms in and tells everybody to get the hell out in five minutes or he's not responsible for what happens. And man, we split quick." He thought for a second, "Nobody gave a damn about drunk driving back then. And somehow this enormous freshman lineman is in the john or out in the dark or something, and he's left behind. And Oby's stuck with him. And this kid is way drunk, staggering drunk. Oby manages to somehow maneuver him into the gunner seat of his car and drives away, headed for Burgfort. Now, you gotta know that Oby loved his car. It was always immaculate, inside and out. And, of course, with the car bouncing around through the curves on the back roads, the kid gets sick and blows chunks all over himself, all over Oby, the car, everything. Just sprayed cookies everywhere. Jesus."

Steph and I were howling with laughter.

"Always remember," Rotz said with finger in the air, "no good turn goes unpunished."

He paused and continued, "But, you know, Oby had been a hell-raiser of the first magnitude when he was an undergrad at Einfahrt. And I like to think that the guys who ran the College, the administration, kinda liked Cotta. They could experience our exploits vicariously, from a safe distance. I picture them secretly laughing at our sheer audacity, if nothing else."

"How did your coach take it?" I asked.

"Oh that's another deal. Lou liked to kill us for that party. He called Rory and Rookie in and ripped 'em new ones."

I thought to myself, well, yeah. If there was an accident waiting to happen, it was Cotta. Cotta House was the fuzz on the lollipop, the worm in the tequila, the sand in the Vaseline, the ants at the family picnic, the rattlesnake in the tea party. It was a lodestone for whatever was floating around loose and crazy.

And I wondered what I was doing drifting into orbit around it.

14. THANKSGIVING

Thursday morning I set the table for the feast. I let Rotz and Steph sleep in. I'd left the sleeping arrangements up to her, had carried Rotz upstairs. She knew the house well, and that was not a hill I wanted to die on. I heard the two of them padding about on the second floor. It was comforting.

Early in the afternoon I went to the Fat Friar Restaurant to pick up the turkey dinner I'd ordered. I brought the food back, put it in serving dishes, took it to the table, lit the candles, and called the troops. They were bright-eyed and bushy-tailed.

There, as soft sunlight streamed through the dining room's bay windows, we had succulent turkey and all the trimmings, all the stuff probably rare at Peaceful Pastures, like real potatoes and gravy. There were rich, creamy casseroles and cranberry sauce. I opened two bottles of wine, a red and a white. Rotz ate with gusto, but also with impeccable manners. Steph was her usual delicate and petite nibbler. She ate like a bird, had been watching her weight, eating healthy, ever since I could remember.

We didn't speak much, just enjoyed the moment. It was completely elegant, in its way, and peaceful, human nature at its best. Rotz and Steph talked together as if they'd known each other for a very long time, and in an odd way they probably had. They were fellow travelers. I wasn't especially anxious to admit it, but they made the cutest couple.

Deirdre would have messed it all up, with her officious bustling and constant talking. Not to mention her judgmental attitudes about, well, just about everything.

For dessert we had fresh-made pumpkin pie à la mode topped off with whipped cream. Steph actually broke down and had a sliver. "To be sociable," she said. Her cheeks glowed with contentment, and her eyes were dancing again, like old times.

On occasion, Supreme seemed alone with memories. I brought up the story of the Cotta turkey caper and asked how this meal compared to that one.

"Quieter here," he allowed.

I asked Steph if she'd heard that story. "Oh yes," she giggled. "I've heard them all."

"Not all," Rotz corrected playfully.

It was a dinner I hated to see end. I think all three of us did. We took our time. And when it was finished, Steph helped Rotz to the big couch in the entertainment room. I dialed up one of the many football games aired that afternoon on the wall-screen, and he began watching with enthusiasm. He was soon asleep, however, zonked on that tryptophan in turkey that some think promotes drowsiness.

Steph and I cleared the table and cleaned the kitchen. We chit-chatted. I'd never pried into her affairs, fearing what I might find, so I didn't ask questions, just spoke of everyday things, like the weather and shopping. She volunteered nothing. She wondered how I was doing, and I didn't want to talk about that, so I said everything was fine. When we were finished she joined Rotz, put his head on her thigh, her hand on his chest, and dozed a bit herself.

I left them and went to my room to nap.

That evening, Supreme was invigorated, and we watched the better part of a football game together, drinking beer, snacking. He commented with authority as the action swirled around us, usually pointing out some aspect of the intricacies of the play before the announcers did. He could look at the situation, at a defense, and predict a play call. I asked him how he did it. "The offense takes what the defense gives them," he explained. "The defense can never cover it all. And if you know the defense well, you know the tendencies of the individual players. Where are the weaknesses? There's always a weakness. What can you exploit?"

It was an education. I was beginning to realize that Supreme was, as much as anything, an education. I asked him about the violence.

"You don't feel it," he said. "It feels good when you play, a big hit wakes you up in a way, heightens your senses, makes you alive, more alive."

He told me that many years after his playing days he was the color man for the Einfahrt radio broadcasts of the football games. He was able to predict Einfahrt plays with remarkable accuracy, but this time he confessed it was because the offensive coordinator was in the booth right next to him in the pressbox, calling them. The coach would hold up the playbook and point, so Rotz could see it through the window. People thought he was psychic.

Friday morning we went for a walk, Rotz in his little cart. It was a beautiful day, warm and sunny. The air felt good. We came upon a park. Steph got Supreme on a teeter-totter, then a swing. I sat on a bench and watched. They were children, somehow, still kids. Forever young.

When we got back to the house, we lunched on the leftovers from the banquet. Completely cool. We watched more football that night. It was fascinating, what with Rotz there to explain things for me.

The next morning, after breakfast, Steph helped me tidy up and did their laundry. I helped them pack. We loaded the van and drove off to Iowa. There was much laughter as the miles went by. We chatted about all sorts of things. We got even better acquainted.

And it occurred to me that I had never really known Aunt Stephanie quite like this. All those years… and now, finally, it was as if she were a companion, a peer, not someone who had once taken care of me and now someone I had to take care of. I apologized for taking her back to the institution.

"Oh god, Marv," she said, "I can't thank you enough for PP. That was the best thing you ever did for me."

Rotz thanked me for the Thanksgiving. "Awesome," he said.

I dropped them off, put their bags and Rotz's cart on the loading dock, and watched wistfully as the staff helped the two of them make their way through the door together and into the building.

It wasn't until driving home that it fully hit me: Steph's mind was sharp as a tack.

When Deirdre returned the next day she asked how it had gone.

"Fucking great," I answered. I no longer cared. What I'd spent so many years putting into place, my life, was falling apart.

15. Winter

The heavy snows came early. The Interstates were cleared quickly enough, but the smaller roads took time. On a mid-December Saturday I drove to see Steph and Rotz. The snowfield looked like some enormous Grandma Moses painting, pristine and framed with roads and tree lines. Drifts had socked in the farmyards, climbing up the sides of red barns and white farmhouses, burying evergreens in frosting. The entire tableau glittered in cold, brilliant sunshine. Blue skies…

I arrived at Peaceful Pastures to find that Steph had pretty much moved into Rotz's room. The administrative staff didn't seem to mind. "Whatever Works." It was all fine with me, although I no longer had Supreme to myself so much. But that was OK too.

I'd brought some things Steph had requested so she could decorate the room for Christmas, and while she busied herself with that task, Rotz suggested we repair to the commons area to talk.

When we got there, I said, "Tell me a story, Uncle Supreme." We looked out the window at the snow-covered fields.

He thought for a minute. "OK," he said, "a few short ones. Then I wanna take you somewhere." He was wearing an expensive, black leather jacket I'd never seen before. It was a bit roomy, as he had shrunk over time. In it I could see his former dimensions, his prime.

"Now, remember Bloyers?"

"The bullshitter, right? the Chicago boy."

"The very one, Marv. Good work. Bloyers founded and was the driving force behind The Friday Afternoon Club, the FAC."

"OK," I said, smiling with anticipation, "and what did that do?"

"That was a buncha guys who got together formally to drink on Friday afternoons. They'd go to a local watering hole and drink."

"That was it?"

"That was it, pretty much. They even had officers. Bloyers was president of course, and there was a VP and a secretary and a treasurer. Minutes were taken at every meeting and read back at the next one."

"What was to read back if they just drank?" I asked.

Rotz shook his head. "I know. They did sing. Every meeting began with a ceremonial chorus of the *Wiffenpoof Song*, that old Yale tune which, by the way, is a parody of Kipling's *Gentlemen Rankers*. Did you know that, Marv?" he asked.

I shook my head good-naturedly.

"Anyway, it was all a big spoof, of course," he continued. "I think Bloyers even managed to get a picture of the Club in the College's annual, *The Buttress*. And the club did take field trips to other bars in various towns in the area. Every once in a while the meeting would spill out from the bar into real life, and countless hours were completely blown in mindless, escapist frivolity. So it was that one fine spring Friday afternoon unexpectedly extended far into the night when a bunch of us found ourselves drinking in a basement somewhere in Burgfort and listening to comedy records."

"Whatta ya mean, records?"

"Vinyl albums, Marv, you know, those LPs?"

"Oh yeah..."

"We had great comedians back then. Lenny Bruce of course. Newhart, Shelley Berman..."

Those names meant nothing to me, but it didn't matter. It was the sheer pleasure of Rotz's renderings that I'd come to enjoy as much as anything.

"McVeety was there, and Baity-ro and his friend Ron Ball, who was the Einfahrt Student Body President, and Bloyers and some other guys.

It was great. We drank and laughed until the sun was coming up, at which point reality beckoned and we all started crashing, so it was time to head back to the House and sleep through Saturday.

"Baity-ro had this little blue sports car, a Sunbeam Alpine – a 2-seater rag-top with a kind of ledge for a back seat – and we all climbed on. There was no room for Bloyers, so he jumped on the left front fender, holding his albums in one hand and a bottle of wine in the other. Well, when we got near the House, Baitman took a hard right at speed and Bloyers parted company with the vehicle, was in effect airborne. We watched as he flew halfway across the street, landed on his keister, and slid into the curb."

"Was he hurt?"

"Shit no, he had an enormous ass that cushioned his touch-down. But what I remember most were the showers of sparks that came shooting out from the grommets of his Levis as his derrière skidded across the concrete. He never lost his grip on the records though. More importantly, he didn't spill a drop of wine. He had his priorities in order."

"Was he pissed?"

"Naw, we were all drunk. It was fun." Rotz quickly shifted gears. "There's another Bloyers car story, one that Baity-ro used to tell before he disappeared. Now, the roads around here have improved over the years, but back when we were in college, well, some were dangerous, and none more dangerous than scenic Highway 20. It was a major east-west road that went through Dubuque and into Illinois. It was two-lane, but it also sometimes had a third lane down the middle for passing, and traffic moving in either direction could use it."

"How'd the drivers know which vehicle had the right-of-way in the middle lane?"

"Exactly," he agreed. "That was the problem. There were so many accidents and fatalities on that stretch of highway that the people who drove it regularly got together and put up big billboards warning everybody about the road they were on. Like, the signs read 'Highway 20 Kills' and shit like that. They had skulls and crossbones on them. They were black and white."

"I've never heard of such a thing," I exclaimed.

"Well, I saw those signs," Rotz said, "so I know they were there. Now, do you know what an MG is?"

I thought for a bit but drew a blank.

"MG makes cars, or used to make them. I have no idea what MG stands for. They were British. They were little sports cars, soft tops, no roll bars. I don't think they even had seat belts, although I'd guess you were better off being thrown from the car in an accident, because it would probably disintegrate upon impact. They were death traps. And Bloyers got one from his foster parents, a little green MGB-GT, as I recall, a fastback. It went like hell.

"So it's the end of the school year, May, and Baiter wanted to get to Chicago to see his fiancée and he hitched a ride with Bloyers, who was going home. It was a beautiful day, sunny, and they were heading east on Highway 20 with the top down. They had a cooler in the tiny rear area and were drinking beers. Baity-ro said it happened very fast."

"Oh shit," I said, fearing the worst. I hate slaughter of any kind.

"They're goin' 60, 70 miles an hour when they came up over a hill and were confronted with two semis coming at 'em, side-by-side, like right on 'em. And there were only two lanes. There was nowhere to go but the ditch. Fortunately for them, the ditch was more like a broad embankment at that section of road, a gentle slope, grassy, like a meadow. There were no culverts, no trees, no crossing roadbeds, no telephone poles. So Bloyers drove down the embankment for an instant as the semis passed and then gunned it back up onto the highway. He didn't even have time to slow down."

"Hard to believe," I said, "the good fortune."

"Tell me about it," he said. "The whole thing took maybe three seconds. Baity-ro was stunned. He said it was like you weren't sure what had just happened, like a dream. And he looked at Bloyers, and Bloyers looked back at him and laughed and held up his beer can and said, 'Never spilled a drop.' Which was true, he hadn't. He'd done the whole maneuver with one hand on the wheel."

"They'da been killed," I said.

"They'da been atomized," Rotz agreed. "All the crazy stuff we did and only Wolfy died. We all coulda been killed at some point. I have no idea how we made it through."

"Glad you did," I smiled.

"Me too." He pursed his lips with that slight, wistful smile. "Vehicles were a constant source of intrigue for Cotta men. None of us were what you'd call mechanics, but we all had cars. And shit was always going wrong with them. The Baitman pulled up to the House one perfect autumn afternoon in that Sunbeam as we were hanging out enjoying the day. A Sunbeam was another little death trap of a British sports car. He had the top down and made a left turn into the grassy, gravel area that passed for the House driveway. Unfortunately, he didn't quite clear a huge, oncoming Pontiac sedan, which pretty much destroyed his right front, caved in the wheel and all that. It was like a ballet. A very big crash was produced, lotsa noise, impressive. We all applauded and cheered from the front porch, and Baity-ro, showman that he was, got out and bowed dramatically to us, as if taking a curtain call. He even motioned to the guy who was driving the Pontiac as if to acknowledge his contribution. Course, that guy was out of his car and storming towards him, really pissed, but there wasn't much he could do except get the insurance information, what with all these big guys standing around. Baiter claimed he was the injured party, since he'd been hit, when it was clearly his fault."

"How'd that turn out?"

"Insurance paid. No problem. The insurance industry was our constant companion. Then there was the day Beatle pulled in with a brand-new used car. And he was always a cocky little bastard to begin with, but that day his chest was especially pumped up. It was a Chevy sedan, this boat of a convertible, with three on the column."

"Um…"

"Yes, Marv, I know. It had three gears and the gearshift was on the right side of the steering column, between the wheel and the dash," he patiently explained. "Neutral was in the middle, reverse was back and up, first was back and down. To go from first to second, you brought the gearshift up to neutral, let it snap forward, and then pushed it up to second. Third was straight down from second. Got it?"

"Sort of."

"OK, well Beatle was just proud as punch, and he told us all to stand out on the porch and watch him accelerate down the street, running the gears. He wanted to show us how he could get rubber in second, or some asinine thing that none of us gave a shit about, but there we were anyway. And Beatle has the top down, and he comes roaring up the street in first and makes a massive shift to second as he neared the House, slamming the gearshift up the column with all his might, whereupon the gearshift comes off in his hand…"

"What?"

"Yeah, just broke off," Rotz laughed. And the car kinda goes 'galump, clang, galump' and comes to a rapid and complete stop."

I was laughing. "Oh, it was funny," said Rotz, "instant and utter deflation. Beatle's sitting there in a dead car with his right arm frozen straight in the air, holding the stick – stunned, like he can't believe it, absorbing the debacle. Oh god." He paused until I was composed.

"Then there was Fred, who came back to school one year with a new used red Triumph, yet another death-trap, rag-top British sports car. And it's autumn, a beautiful, sunny afternoon, and he loans the car to his roommate Woody so Woody can take Berfel's girl for a ride in the country. Apparently, the two were old high school friends. And they're tooling along a back road, top town, when the steering wheel suddenly comes off in Woody's hands. He hits the brakes and the car veers sharply into the right ditch and runs headlong into a telephone pole. The pole snaps off and begins to fall back onto the car. Just before it lands on the passengers, and it mighta killed somebody, the wires hold and it stops, hanging there, suspended in mid-air. Woody and the girl scrambled out. The Triumph was completely totaled. When Woody gets back to the House, Ferd says to him, 'That's what you get for drivin' my girl around.' Rotz smiled, "No sympathy."

"You guys were accident-prone," I said.

"We lacked caution and restraint." He brightened, "Hey, but speaking of vehicles, you ready to go?" he asked.

"Where to?"

"A surprise. Steph knows about it. She said to let her stay here and decorate." He rolled to the front desk, took his cane out of the cart, stood up, and signed out. I'd become a kind of fixture there, I guess, and the lady at the desk asked Rotz if he was going with me. She told him I didn't look very reliable. "I know," Rotz assured her, "I'll be extra careful."

I laughed easily as I helped him through the front doors to my car. "Is it far? I asked.

"Downtown Burgfort, the metropolis," he replied.

16. Captain America

Supreme directed me up Main Street to an ancient, sprawling, one-story building that looked as though it might once have been an auto dealership. It had become a car repair place. Vehicles old and new in various states of disrepair if not abandonment were scattered around the lot, most buried by piles of snow that had been plowed up to make room for vehicles that actually ran. Rotz had me drive around to the back. I parked where he told me and got out. I helped him through the slush and into the service office. It was cluttered with auto parts, papers, computers, devices of all kinds, and general grime. The walls were decorated with girlie calendars that advertised various car and tool products. I only saw one that had dates for the current year on it.

Behind the desk sat what I took to be the proprietor, a large man about my age, unshaven, in bib overalls and a T-shirt. Rotz took care of the introduction. "Marv, meet my friend Jake." I shook his big, calloused hand and smiled.

"So you're Marv," Jake greeted me with a big, raspy voice and a slight southern accent. "You're a lucky man." He looked at Rotz, "How're ya doin?" he asked.

"Hangin' in there," Rotz allowed, "better than I deserve."

"Can't top that," Jake said. "Shall we go see if it's still there?"

"Why not," Rotz replied.

Jake led us through a hallway into a small room with a wide exterior door. He turned on an overhead florescent light. In the middle of the concrete floor, a tarp covered a large lump of something. He carefully took it off to reveal a motorcycle. An authoritative motorcycle. "Ain't that sweet?" he rasped.

It sparkled. It had so much shiny chrome that it was difficult to fathom at first. It had big handlebars that were higher than most cycles. It had seats for two, a driver and a rider. It had beautiful black leather saddlebags slung under the back seat. The gas tank was painted in red and white stripes, with a corner of deep blue dotted with white stars. I looked at Rotz in amazement. "What is it?" I said.

Jake answered. "Son, that's an *Easy Rider* Harley, circa 1969."

This told me nothing.

"There was a movie," Jake kindly explained, "called *Easy Rider*. It was the seminal biker flick of that era. Ever heard of it?"

I vaguely remembered hearing something about it. I wasn't sure though.

"Well," Jake was patient, "it starred Peter Fonda, Henry's son. And Dennis Hopper. And a young, unknown actor named Jack Nicholson. It kinda wrote the book on bikers, for that time and place."

"It was anti-establishment," Rotz chimed in, "but in an interesting way. The lead character called himself *Captain America*, and if I recall, Hopper directed it."

"Yes, I believe he did," growled Jake. "You gotta dial that flick up, Marv. It's important."

"You mean this is the actual bike from the movie?" I asked.

"Not the very one they used, but Supreme here had a friend in, I wanna say California..." He deferred to Rotz.

"Newport Beach," Rotz chimed in.

"... made a few replicas like it for the general public. This is a classic bike, Marv, a chopper, understand that, means it's been modified, chopped up. It didn't come like this outta the box. It's a 1951 Harley Davidson Panhead, 55 horses and 4800 RPM. It'll go at least 100. And it's customized." Jake walked to the handlebars. "Look, this is what's called a *rigid wishbone* frame, and it's laid back. These front forks are extended a foot." He walked to the rear of the bike, "The buddy seat upholstery is all folded under."

"Jake's been working on it. He put in directionals," Rotz said.

I tried to show the proper respect. "It's got directionals?"

"And an electric starter. And I overhauled it recently," Jake added.

And then Rotz said with a big smile, "It's yours, Marv."

I didn't grasp the situation. I fumbled.

"This belongs to Rotz," Jake said, "and he's giving it to you."

I was speechless.

"You might could thank him, for openers," Jake commanded.

"But, well, sure, thanks, but what am I gonna do with this? I don't know the first thing about it. You keep it Rotz."

"Marv," Jake was now quite firm, "don't look a gift horse in the mouth, especially this one. I'd kill for this iron."

"What am I gonna do with it?" Rotz said, leaning heavily on his cane. "Besides, Jake'll give you lessons, teach you how to ride."

Before I was able to protest, Jake cut me off. "We'll start you out on little scooters, easy. We'll work our way up to this one."

"Dammit, Supreme," I said, "I'm gonna talk you outta this."

"Don't even try," he said, "he who dies with the most toys is still dead."

I shook my head.

"The deal is done, the paperwork's done," Rotz insisted, "all you gotta do is sign it, Marv. Then he asked Jake how it was running.

"Smooth as silk, I take it out whenever it's nice. Tiptop shape. Goes like a motherfucker."

"Picks 'em up and lays 'em down," Rotz laughed. "There ya go, Marv, all wrapped up. An early Christmas present."

He thanked Jake; I thanked Jake. We got back into the car and Rotz directed me to a local bar. An old neon sign out front said *The Hawk*. I parked the van and helped Supreme to the front door.

17. JOE'S HAWK

We went in and sat in a booth. The place was deserted. It was spotless and neat, a period piece in a pleasant way, decorated in roughly the same hues as Rotz's little cart pennant. I wasn't sure if a kind of off-pink and ultraviolet were the intended colors or if everything had simply faded over time. Words like "Teutons" and "Fighting Teutons" were all over the place, along with memorabilia, old football helmets and jerseys, medieval knight trimmings, and so forth. There was an athletic *Wall of Fame*.

A spry, thin old man came over smartly, bringing two draft beers. He set them down in front of us and asked to see Rotz's ID. They laughed. "Meet Joe," he said, "owns the place. *El Patron.*"

Pleasantries were exchanged, and Joe walked back to the bar where he busied himself cleaning things. I took the opportunity to stare across the table at *Rotzinger Number One Supreme*. He was in his element at last, sitting in a bar having a beer. "Joe and I graduated together," he began, "and this place is where all the reunions were." He took a breath. "No more of that though, Joe and I are the only ones left. And he wasn't even Cotta, he lived in a real house, where the business guys were."

"I'm sorry, Rotz," I said, "about your House brothers."

"Yeah, they're all gone. Cancer and heart problems mostly. No one murdered, thank god, no big explosions, no dismemberments. Nothing special. Just time marching on." He caught himself, "Oh wait, Rookie died in some kind of bowling accident."

"How could that be?"

"I dunno, never looked into it. The Buffalo lived a long time, had an iron constitution. He always maintained he'd had a blessed life and was ready to go anytime. Great attitude. Unbelievable. He began to say he'd made falling down a way of life. Smoke, drank, and ate hearty until a major illness caught up with him, and when he made it through that he cleaned up completely, reformed. Shortly thereafter, though, we lost him. But he never lost his sense of humor, and we didn't either."

"A good way to work it," I said.

"Yup." Rotz took a swallow of beer. "Oh, and Beatle died fucking his voluptuous wife."

"You're kidding."

"No," he chuckled, "a massive coronary. It's a moment I guess you'd describe as 'dripping with bittersweet irony'... and probably some other stuff."

"What a way to go."

"The very best," said Rotz. Then his face fell a bit. He leaned forward and lowered his voice, "Marv, just so you know, the Grim Reaper is after me now. Tough being this old."

"I'm sure," I said, "but you look terrific."

"Marv, listen... it's the ticker." He pointed to his chest.

"But there's so much they can do these days," I protested. "A transplant?"

"Nope, already had one years ago. The doctors have advised me. It's systemic, too much is wrong. I got more stents in me than Heinz has pickles. Maybe your grandchildren will be able to get through this kinda stuff, but it's too late for me." He added, "Don't tell Steph."

"But it seems like she's your fountain of youth."

Supreme looked down and thought so long this time I was certain I'd said something wrong again. He finally looked up and asked, "How well do you know your Aunt Stephanie?"

I told him I thought we were pretty close, not soul mates, of course.

"She faked dementia," he said. "Did you know that?"

I was astounded, but I instantly knew he was right. I protested nonetheless, "Aw c'mon Rotz, why would she do something like that?"

"To get away from your wife. She told me she couldn't breathe around her."

"Why wouldn't she just tell me?"

"Where else was she to turn? You were all she had. Deirdre's your wife. That's a legal relationship. Far too risky for Steph. And see, she read an article in some, like, AARP Magazine or something, about all the sex going on in assisted living venues…"

"But I thought it was *my* idea to get her here."

He leaned back. His voice grew calming, soothing. "Marv, sweetheart, *boychick*… it's *never* our idea; it's always theirs. Babes just let us *think* it's our idea. You gotta know that by now."

I was doing my best to absorb this latest shot as he continued.

"She used to be a professional stripper. Did you know *that?*" he asked.

"Say what?" I stammered.

"Yeah, out in Oregon, she told me she did it for a long time."

My mind was too busy to form actual words. Our suspicions, since Steph had been living so well with no visible means of support, had always been that she was involved in prostitution. Mere stripping was a bit of a relief, sort of. Until I remembered it was generally assumed that ladies in that field tended to multi-task.

Rotz interrupted my thoughts. "You all right?" he asked.

"Processing," I said.

His spirits lifted. He gesticulated earnestly for emphasis, became more engaged than I'd ever seen him get. "There's nothing *wrong* with stripping, Marv. It has a rich, cultural history – Salome, her dance of the seven veils, that's in the Bible for chrissake. And burlesque! Gypsy Rose Lee! It's *art* Marv, so factor that into the equation. And Steph is really good at it. I mean, she works out in the PP exercise room, actually lifts free weights, so she can be a better stripper. It's her calling. She loves it. She's a born exhibitionist, Marv, god makes such things. What're ya gonna do?"

My mind was spinning. I mumbled, half to myself, "So that's why she got that full body tuck a few years back." Then out loud, "You know, Supreme, I paid for that surgical, cosmetic make-over of hers." I found myself rambling on, "And those aren't implants, ya know, they just lifted and tightened 'em." What was I *saying*? It was like I was proud of it. I took a massive swallow of beer, wiped my mouth with my sleeve.

"Not to mention the ass," Rotz said with genuine respect, as though evaluating a Van Gogh.

"Yeah," I acknowledged, "I know, I know, I *noticed*." Something in me wouldn't stop. "Then after that the dermatologist did the injections with that hormonal stuff, it's like she got new skin, no wrinkles, amazing..." I caught myself. What had I done...?

"I thank you," he laughed, "the guys thank you." He clapped his hands softly.

"Good god," I said, "you mean there's a crowd?"

"Well, strippers aren't much fun in empty rooms, Marv. Of course there's a crowd. Peaceful Pastures does have a nice party room downstairs, ya know, communal hot tub and everything. They even put in a stage and a pole for Steph, her specifications. Nice lighting, flashing and dark, then that sexy music blasting on those speakers they got in the walls... so orderlies off-duty drop in, and nurses."

"You mean there's *women*?!" I was yelling.

"Marv," he chided me, down boy, "naturally there's women. It's a *partyyyyy*!"

My initial misgivings about the place had now been confirmed in spades. I moaned in frustration. "How many?"

"How many what?"

"People."

"Jeez, I dunno. I'm not good at estimating crowds. A hundred? Townies sneak in I think. Doctors. They roll bedridden people in there."

"What??!!"

"It's loud, Marv, it's excitement! The lap dances she gives, oh baby!! She gets all the ladies doin' 'em!! Hey, you know that new synthetic morphine stuff they got for pain killers?"

"I've heard of it, I think," I replied without enthusiasm.

"It works great! It's a *ball* Marvin." He raised his glass.

"That's what I'm afraid of."

"Listen," he said. He was consoling, "Anyone who doesn't appreciate a good stripper has never watched a rose open."

I blinked.

"Roses take a week, they're tantalizing, very seductive. Relax, Marv. It's a natural thing."

I was trying to find the right question. "Does she, um, I mean, what is she left with?"

Rotz was nonplussed. He stared sideways before looking at me. "Well *yes*, why *wouldn't* she take it all off? She's a fuckin' *stripper!*" He smiled and looked off into the distance. "God, she's got the cutest stuff. Loves to show it off."

I couldn't take it. Half of me was disgusted, and the other half was hurt because I hadn't ever been invited to one of those things. I was twisted up inside.

He seemed to enjoy my obvious discomfort. He leaned closer and whispered with admiration, "Steph is big on group sex. She's an outstanding performer, really works a room, if you know what I mean."

I gagged on a swallow of beer, coughed, wiped up with a paper napkin as I talked. "Dammit, spare me the details, Rotz," I yelled, "it's my fucking aunt!"

He was actually taken aback. He shushed me, looked over my shoulder for Joe. He got quieter. Leaned into the table. "OK Marv, calm down a sec. Awright now just think, see if you can work through this. Can you maybe try to tell me what exactly you feel is wrong with it? Think. I mean, stripping's legal, right?"

"I dunno. What are the laws around here?"

"It's legal Marv."

"Um."

"And we're all adults at PP, *old* adults." He was actually pleading. His face took on a look of abject pity. "Haven't we earned some silly little piece of actual fun and entertainment before we're out the door for good?"

I was bending. "I suppose..." What the hell did I know...

"So find something wrong."

I was stumped.

"It isn't as if we're corrupting the nation's youth."

I sighed; I was resigned to it. "It's my fucking aunt," I said again, flatly.

Rotz sniffed. "Well, I rest my case."

"Um."

"It's your hang-up. But I'd get over it." He paused. It was quiet. "Marv," he finally said, "look at me."

I obeyed. I looked directly into his eyes. I'd never done that. I'd avoided them. I think I didn't want to see what was looking back at me, didn't want to see my future or his past. But there we finally were, face to face. And I saw all of it, the loneliness of age, the pain, the sorrows, the warrior, the patriarch, the joy and power of youth, the wistfulness, the laughter. I saw life, I guess...

"Listen Marv," he stared at me until he was certain I was focused on him. Then he said, "Experience everything except incest and murder."

I think he was serious, but there was that little pursing-of-the-lips thing of his.

He held the moment for but a short time, then brightened. He lifted his beer again. "Enjoy life Marv, it's later than you think."

I suddenly remembered another problem, "Oh shit," I blurted, "don't tell Deirdre I paid for Steph's body lift, that surgery stuff."

"How'm I gonna tell her? I don't even *know* her. You worry too much." We both thought to ourselves for a bit. He broke the silence. "Hey?"

"Yeah?"

"How is that your wife doesn't know you spent a chunk of money on Steph? You been holding out on her?"

He had me there. He'd landed on it. Probably dumb luck, but here we were. "Well," I said, "early on in the marriage, I got some kinda cold feet, after the kids were born and she had me dead to rights…" I caught myself, "you should pardon the expression."

"Jesus, it's OK."

"Nobody knows, only you. Oh, and Steph of course, but I swore her to silence. She came to me in tears. She hated what age had done to her face and body. She showed me this ad from this surgical place that could tighten up skin. It really wasn't very expensive. I felt for her. She's so sweet, and I love her very much." I was getting emotional as I recalled her unhappiness.

Rotz signaled to Joe for another beer for me. "It's all right, Marv, you did a good thing. Hell, I'm not judging you for what you do in a marriage. Marriages are to be survived. All's fair in love and war… and police… and marriage."

I took a deep couple of swallows of beer and pumped up my courage. "Just don't tell anyone about this." I instinctively glanced around and lowered my voice. "See, I got this account I set up years ago; it's secret. A little bit here and there, interest builds in it, then investments are made too, mutual funds, you know how that works. It has added up very well. I did it because Deirdre kept threatening divorce, it's one of the ways she always got her way. She'd say she would take the kids and leave, with me paying child support. And I couldn't trust her to give the child support to the kids, so I kept some money aside for them. But we never got divorced, miraculously, and I never needed it. I told Deirdre that Steph's health insurance covered everything. Christ, what a lie that was. All Dee had to do was dial up a Medicare phone bot to nail me, and maybe she did. But she never mentioned it. She's always busy with other stuff."

"Marv, what do you do? I mean, for work."

The conversation was going from bad to worse. It was like a confessional. Father Supreme. "I'm not sure I know anymore. I used to know, years ago. I'm with a consulting firm. And they provide me daily assignments and then keep changing iDevices on me, so I sit and play with whatever iDoohickey they saddle me with that day, and I move shit around, and they keep paying me. It pays very well."

"Can you give me a hint with this, at what you do? I mean, at least a domain."

"Medical technology, a lotta stuff going down these days with those organ-farm things. Tissue regeneration. You know, our grandkids may never die, they'll live forever in some watery, sci-fi inferno of a planet. Hell, my doctor tells me I could live to be 110, maybe longer."

"Got any hobbies?" he asked.

"Not really, kinda workin' on that."

"You'll need some," he smiled. "Lotta time to kill."

"They say 150 is no longer out of the question."

"Well, more power to 'em. I tell you though, I'm not so concerned with my body wearing out. It's my mind is worn out, that's the issue."

"Why?"

"I get so tired of watching people do the same dumb things over and over. There's no societal memory these days, if there ever was. People forget from year to year, decade to decade. It's hopeless. It exhausts me, the complete stupidity."

"Oh, yeah, I know whatcha mean."

"I've watched this country dumb itself down beyond recognition. There's no hope. There's no depth. If they can't say it in five seconds, they don't say it. It's all superficial. Enormously complex problems are reduced to a sound bite. Our government is run by crazy people, complete idiots."

I nodded; he went on.

"There's so much gluttony, so much greed. Nobody gives a shit about anybody else. It's every person for his or her self. They give us old people a fancy name like 'senior citizens' and then dump us off and forget about us. My grandmother lived to be 100 and always lived with her children. She was cared for by family until she died."

"I'm sorry," I said. "Guilty." And I raised my hand slightly.

"I'm you, ya know," he said, "if you're lucky."

"Whattaya mean?"

"You're either gonna die young or grow old. Personally, I think six feet over beats six feet under any day."

"Oh." He was right about that.

"But enougha me, what about you, Marv? You? You keep dodging that one."

"I'm swamped in all the data, that's for sure. It comes in from everywhere, all the time. I can't think straight, all the devices, all the communication."

"Yeah, well, I never bought into all that shit to begin with. I got off that train when they started that texting shit."

I laughed. "I shoulda done that too," I said.

"But that's not what I mean, Marv. I mean you, personal-like, where you live."

"I've always made good money, Rotz. And I've taken care of it too."

"I'm sure you have; you've been a fine son and husband and father. And nephew to Steph. What have you ever done for yourself, though? Ever had any fun?"

We had hit it now, the heart of the matter. This is what had been keeping me up nights ever since, well, ever since I'd found Cotta, wondering what might have been, what I could have done. "I dunno Rotz, I feel trapped sometimes, cornered."

"Well, forgive me again, none of my business, but you feel trapped because you are."

And then it dawned on me. I'd known all of this for a long time, just hadn't admitted it to myself. Supreme had become my way out. My subconscious had been taking care of me.

18. TESTING

I leaned against the corner of the booth, lost in thought. He carefully nursed his first beer. Joe came over, bringing a new round for me and some fries for the table. He pointed out the window. "There's the old campus," he said, "just down the street. Those beautiful stone buildings. All empty now. Except for the computers."

"This was the great student hangout," Rotz said.

"Have you heard all the Cotta stories?" I asked Joe.

"Not yet," Supreme shot in.

"He won all the puking contests," Joe said. "He was a great competitor, and he'd had to make a huge adjustment. He'd grown up trying to keep it down, then they changed the rules on him. God, that Cotta kitchen would stink."

I was a stranger in a strange land.

"I have a story," Joe said.

"Let's hear it." Rotz was as avid a listener as a teller.

"The best test-cheating story I ever came across," Joe began. "This guy, one of my house brothers, Teddy, shows up totally unprepared for a final in a religion course. It's a required course, he needs it to graduate, and if he flunks the test, well… hell to pay. The final is a couple essay questions and he's got the usual two hours or so to write something. He hasn't a clue what the answers are, but he sits there writing his buns off, writing doodly, while the prof occasionally wanders around the room to

135

check progress. As time is running out, Teddy realizes he's written total crap and will flag the course, and somehow this idea borne of desperation comes to him. He takes a fresh piece of paper and writes a letter to his mother, just a newsy little chat, nothing special. When it's time to turn in his test, he puts the letter to his mom on the pile."

This was making no sense to me.

Joe continued. "He gets out of the classroom and immediately runs to the library, finds a reference book or two pertaining to the test questions, and writes excellent answers for them. For all I know, he copied pieces directly from the books. He then puts them in an envelope addressed to his mom, hustles to the Burgfort post office, and drops the letter in the mail box.

"That night, he calls the prof at his home and pretends to be distressed. The prof is sympathetic. Teddy tells him he thinks he made a big mistake – instead of turning in his test, he turned in a letter to his mom. He fears he mailed the test answers to her. It was a mixup."

I got it; it clicked in, was perfect. I smiled.

Joe warmed to the denouement. "Well, the prof, no stranger to problem-solution, asks Ted how long he thinks it'll take for the letter to get to his mom. Teddy figures a couple days, max. Religion profs were always desperate to forgive anyway, and this prof was a kindly man, so he suggested he simply call Teddy's mom in a few days and ask her to read the test to him over the phone. Naturally, Teddy is relieved, gives him his mom's phone number, and thanks him profusely. As an added touch, he wonders if the prof would be kind enough to post the letter to his mom. Well, easily done, anything to help a student. Teddy gives the guy his parents' address and promises to pay for the stamp, and that was it."

Rotz applauded. "Did it work?" he asked.

"Miraculously," Joe replied, "it did. Religion guys were so trusting. Ted passed the course with flying colors."

"Took some real balls, that," Rotz said with admiration. "That's inspired."

"Teddy was in dire straights," Joe said with a big smile. "Necessity is the mother…"

I was nonplused. That was a major fraud. That was in a whole different league. He'd involved his sainted momma.

I finished my beer while we nibbled on the fries. I offered to pay the tab, but Rotz insisted on covering it.

"I'll get the tip," I said.

"Ya know…" he said, "whenever I hear that word I think about the circumciser's apprentice."

"The circumciser's apprentice?"

"Yeah, he got eight bucks an hour plus tips."

I laughed.

"So put a hefty tip on the table," he jovially commanded, "and let's blow this pop stand."

We got in the van and drove around the campus. Rotz was the tour guide. The football field was still there, under a pile of snow. He thought they used it for high school games. He showed me where Cotta used to be. It was a vacant lot.

"After us, the flies," he stated reverently, his finger in the air, as he stared out the window at it.

"Maybe all the ghosts on that property wouldn't let them build anything," I said.

We headed back to Peaceful Pastures slowly. It had been an overwhelming two hours. "How can I ever repay you for that bike?" I asked softly as I walked beside his little cart on the way to his room.

"Use it," he said. "Learn how to drive it and use it. I don't know anybody else who would use it. My daughter would just sell it. So would Jake. I want to know who's on it."

I promised him I'd learn how to ride it.

He stopped at his door. "Oh, and Marv," he said, looking up at me very seriously, "there's hope for you yet. I see your hair's gettin' longer."

He'd noticed.

We walked into the room. Steph was still decorating. It had become very Christmassy. For some reason, I was expansive.

"Did Supreme get you liquored up?" she laughed. "Did you get my nephew stewed?"

"Not so's it'd show," Rotz replied.

"Is he in a good mood, darlin'?"

"Ask him, baby."

"Marv, can we come home with you for Christmas? We have nowhere else to go." She flirtatiously batted her eyes at me, an old habit of hers.

Emboldened by the beer, the Harley, and the mood, I replied, "I'll clear it with Deirdre. If she doesn't like it, I'll take you guys to the Bahamas. How's that?"

"You two should go out carousing more often," she said, and giggled.

I had a lot of new input to deal with. As I drove away from Burgfort in the late afternoon, I flashed on Steph's infectious titter, wondering why it was stuck in my head. The answer came to me quickly. It was when I was a little boy, fourth grade perhaps, just home from school and bounding up the stairs in what I thought was an empty house, running down the carpeted hall for the bathroom to whiz...

I burst in the door without knocking just as Aunt Stephanie was stepping out of the shower. She was reaching for a towel, was as startled as I, and I stopped in my tracks not two feet from her. I remember staring up, stunned and open-mouthed, at her perfect breasts – I didn't dare look straight ahead. She was all wet and statuesque, like a goddess. I recall the air being filled with steam that diffused the light. It was like some kind of religious thing, a nimbus around her body.

Instead of covering up, she wrapped the towel around her hair and said something like, "Well, you were gonna see a girl sooner or later. I guess now is the time." And she spread her arms out and went, "Ta da..." like she was modeling a dress. And there was that playful giggle...

I was mortified and embarrassed at the same time that I was fascinated. I couldn't look away, couldn't move, was afraid to stay and afraid to go. "I'm, I'm, I'm sorry," I stuttered, gazing at her, about to cry. I figured I was in big trouble sure.

"Aw Marvin sweety," she soothed in that soft, husky voice of hers, "it isn't your fault, it's OK, you didn't do anything wrong." And she took my head gently and held it lovingly against her wet tummy. She patted me on the shoulder, reassuringly. "It's all normal, don't worry," she said, "accidents happen." She smelled of perfumed shampoo.

Then she reached up for the towel. Her hair fell as she took the soft, white cloth, wrapped it around her body, and nonchalantly walked out, shutting the bathroom door behind her, leaving me standing there all by myself with an inexplicable stiffy.

I had been conflicted about that encounter, and about Auntie Steph, ever since.

19. Christmas

As it turned out, Deirdre was only too happy to head to the bosom of her family for Christmas. And our kids weren't coming home. This was the alternate year for both; they would spend the holidays with in-laws in Missouri and Texas. We gold-dust triplets had my place to ourselves.

There were waist-high piles of snow on the shoulders of the road to Burgfort. I didn't trust the GPS pilot, what with all the ice, so I drove it myself. I had come to know every turn.

I stopped off at Jake's shop and found him there, asked if I could look at the Harley and that was no problem. I took off the tarp and studied it. It was without blemish. I was taken in by the sheer beauty of it, all that polished chrome, the airbrushed paint job. I was still trying to figure out how it could possibly be mine. Jake was obviously envious, but congenial nonetheless. Turned out he and Rotz went way back, used to ride their bikes together to the Dakota Sturgis Falls Biker Festivals and on other, longer trips. They would camp out, he told me, smoke dope under the stars in the southwestern deserts. Talk themselves to sleep around the campfire. That was when Rotz was a big CEO, after his wife died and his daughter had moved west. Those odysseys to the wilderness were much-needed respites for him because he was forced to be very responsible in real life. He allowed himself the luxury of unwinding only in distant private.

Peaceful Pastures was festive and bustling, filled with holiday spirit. Rotz and Steph were packed and ready when I got to their room. They had lots of gifts, all wrapped in colorful paper with bright ribbons and bows and loaded in shopping bags. I took the stuff to the van, they signed out, and we were off to the city.

Our house didn't look festive at all. Deirdre hadn't decorated and I'd been busy. Besides, I'm not much for that kind of stuff. She and I had exchanged meaningless presents perfunctorily as she was leaving.

But even though the house was unadorned, it was clean. And I'd ordered a Christmas Eve dinner with all the trimmings from The Friar, and I'd managed to find, assemble, and put up the fake tree we stored in the basement. It had lights on it, and decorations from over the years, family stuff. I had put my presents to the two of them under it.

There was plenty of wine and beer on hand, and other spirits. And ersatz logs for the fire.

We had a couple of days before Christmas, so I took Supreme and Steph out shopping one afternoon to a big nearby mall. Rotz rolled around in his cart, Stephanie fairly floated on the delights of the season. They didn't buy much, mostly little silly things. It didn't matter. There was a children's choir singing carols in the central plaza where Santa sat on a golden throne. It was the way it should always be.

Snow fell Christmas Eve, a blizzard. I'd managed to get the meal just before the first flakes started to come down. We ate by candlelight with the tree in the background, holiday music softly playing from the entertainment center and a fire in the hearth. We had sugar-cured baked ham and new potatoes and veggies, a salad of Romaine hearts with chunks of lobster. The wine was delightful and danced with reflections. We forgot about the world, save for glances out the window at the thick snowflakes and gathering drifts. The wind blew, howled occasionally. It just made things cozier.

After dinner, we rested for a while, sipping wine, and then opened presents. I gave each of them the newest iWhatchamacallit so we could be in closer touch. Steph gave Rotz a bunch of gifts, as if sheer numbers were the greatest value. He got clothing, books, trinkets, anything that had caught her eye.

She gave me a cornucopia of dial-ups for movies from the Sixties. I'm trying to remember titles… *Midnight Cowboy, They Shoot Horses Don't They?, Cool Hand Luke, Gimme Shelter, Butch Cassidy and the Sundance Kid*, and of course, *Easy Rider*. And music too, compilations from Credence Clearwater Revival, Elvis, the Beatles, The Byrds, Janis Joplin, Hendrix, The Staple Singers, Chicago, Tracy Nelson, Marvin Gaye, Bob Dylan, Joni Mitchell, The Band, on and on… "Homework!" she playfully shrieked as I studied the great list.

He gave her only one gift, but it was immense – a diamond ring, a huge rock. She wasn't expecting it. She cried. It even fit her, although he pointed out there was a jeweler near Burgfort who could get it just right if need be. I tell you, that was a moment. She hugged him for the longest time. We sat there, not speaking, listening to the Christmas music softly wafting in. We savored the candlelight and the sparkling little bulbs from the tree, with the snow falling out the windows and holiday cheer warming the room. And at the heart of it was Steph's big, new diamond, flashing in the shadows.

There was one last gift, for me, from Rotz. It was a Cotta sweatshirt, navy blue with gold lettering, all caps, COTTA. He'd had it made up special.

"Got one for myself too," he said. "We're the last of the best. You're now a Cotta man, it's official."

I mean, it was astonishing. How could a simple sweatshirt touch me like that? "Is there an initiation ceremony?" I joked.

"As a matter of fact there is," he replied, "but it involves testicles and black shoe polish and shaved pubes and so on. We can forego that for the evening, I think." Steph giggled as he went on, "That tradition was probably started by some deeply closeted gay guy years before I got to the House."

We all laughed, and then he got serious. "Just so you know, Marv, and I don't mean to be maudlin here, but the one thing every Cotta man had to be was a good guy. That was basic, that was the hurdle you had to clear. We only took good guys."

It might have been one of the sincerest compliments I had ever received. Or ever would.

We spent the next couple of days holed up. The blizzard paralyzed the city, but that was OK. We had lots of food to eat, beer to drink, and plenty of good movies to watch.

I noticed something interesting about Rotz. He wasn't so sleepy anymore. He had a renewed energy level. I figured it was because he wasn't alone. Someone that he cared about loved him. A good woman will do that, they say. Renewal was always possible.

And another thing, I don't know why I hadn't made the connection sooner – but these were the fucking *flower children*. This is what was left of the *peace-love* generation, what had become of them. These were the kids weaned on rock n roll. They'd gotten on the bus with Little Richard. They were Captain Video and Howdy Doody, Davy Crocket and Lucy, Flash Gordan and Ricky Nelson, the Mouseketeers, JFK and MLK.

They had marched in Selma and on Washington and died in Mississippi and Ohio, and all because they had this crazy notion that everybody was equal, or should be. Ethnicity or sex or even age didn't matter so much, it was about fulfilling the promise of those fancy words in the American Declaration and Constitution, about equal opportunity. And they also didn't think war had ever been such a good idea and had become a very terrible idea once nukes that could destroy the entire planet were in play. They had seen the earth from the moon early on and understood how fragile it was.

They were test pilots for LSD. They were the product of good diets, physical education, quality public schooling, medical miracles, cosmetic surgery, and so were pushing the envelope of longevity. They had excellent vision and hearing, all their teeth, and most of their faculties. And they were disinclined to go quietly into that good night.

It took three days for the city to dig and shovel and plow its way clear of the mountain of snow that had fallen. We packed the van in the cold on a sunny day and headed to Peaceful Pastures. Rotz and Steph were anxious to get back to their home, that little room, and just relax together. The mood was still festive – leftover Christmas joy. Along the way I asked Rotz if he had any good Christmas stories.

"Not really," he said, "everyone went home for the holidays. I do remember one Christmas break, I came back to the House early to get some studying done. That was when they still ended the semester after the holidays. So I had a term paper to diddle with, and I wanted to cram for finals. It was always difficult to do school work in Cotta, what with all the shit that was constantly going on. So I got to the House one bitterly cold Saturday night a few days before classes were to start again. I had clean clothes and sheets from home and hauled them upstairs to my room and unpacked.

"The place was deserted, dark, totally quiet, almost spooky. I made my bed, put all my clean stuff in the chest of drawers, and sat at my desk to start studying. It was an unsullied space in time, nearly midnight. It was heaven really, the silence. And then I heard front door crash open and two guys came clambering into the House, talking loudly. They stumbled around, thudded up the stairs, and went to the bathroom, where they ran water in the sink and sounded like they were cleaning up. I recognized the voices, Berfel and Hoss. They were drunk and in a hurry.

"I decided to be very quiet in hopes they would just leave or go to bed. Then I could get back to work. No such luck however. Ferd had probably seen the light in my window from outside, and he came and banged his fist on my door. I opened it. He looked terrible. His eyes were bleary. He said, as sincerely and seriously, as authoritatively, as I'd ever heard him speak, 'If anyone asks you if you've seen us tonight, tell 'em you didn't. I think we mighta killed somebody.' Then he shut the door, and the two of them went bounding down the stairs. I remember Fred saying to Hoss, 'Man, the way you just kept pounding that guy's head on the pavement…' They spilled out the front door and all was quiet again.

"I sat there and tried to get back to my paper, but I was now distracted as you might expect. I was trying to figure out what had happened and was planning what I would say if people did show up looking for them. It didn't necessarily have to be the police. It could easily have been a bunch of guys looking for revenge. What if they saw my light and decided to come after me?"

"You could lock the doors," I offered.

"No, we couldn't. We didn't have any keys – Burgfort had no petty theft back then, and people were genuinely afraid of Cotta, for good reason. So I decided the safest thing to do would be to simply turn out the lights and go to sleep. I could tell people I must've gotten back just after they'd come through the House, and that would be that. I could also ignore any knocks at the door."

Stephanie loved Supreme's stories. She always laughed her ass off when he told one. "There went your night of studying," she howled.

"Did anybody die?" I asked, innocently enough.

"Well, I wouldn't be here probably if somebody had. Turned out they'd been in a small town nearby, drinking in some bar, and had gotten into a fight. And Hoss had indeed beat the shit outta some guy, but he lived."

I helped them with their things at the PP loading dock, and made sure they got it all to their room. I took a moment at the front desk on my way out to thank the ladies for letting Rotz and Steph stay together. "No problem," one of them said cheerfully, "Whatever works."

"The best of the Season to all," I said. It had been a very long time since I'd truly had the Christmas spirit. It was some kind of miracle.

Peacefulness, however, proved to be short-lived.

20. Humbly into the Breach

The New Year came and with it a storm from Deirdre. Filled with momentum from her family retreat, she returned determined to get a divorce. In truth, of course, I'd had my fill of it with her and was happy to hear her take the lead in the matter. I had realized at last what I should have known years ago. Because she'd finally made her move, leaving me to play the role of injured party, I was in a position to drive as hard a bargain as I could. In an America where the divorce rate was climbing to 75 percent, divorce was a kind of cottage industry. The Internets were brimming with sites providing legal divorces, all the documents.

In one of the few bursts of fleeting agreement remaining to us, Deirdre and I selected *QuickyVegasDivorce.gov*, a non-profit public service, and went to work. Her fierce feminism, her independent and self-sufficient professionalism, made it easy to dodge any kind of alimony structure.

She didn't want the house, said it was too much for her to handle with all the cleaning. I feigned a great hardship by keeping it, even though I was not ready to part with it. She got her half of the equity we'd built up. The mortgage payments had ended. Basically, I got a free house. She took whatever furniture and furnishings she wanted, and she wanted lots, and moved them into her massive new condo on the other side of town. She took the car; I kept the van.

The way things got divided, the relative ease of it all, it was as if both of us had been planning this in our heads for quite a while.

For all I knew, she had a hidden savings account like mine, but I didn't care. Mine escaped discovery, and I didn't go looking for any skeletons in her closets. Let sleeping dogs lie. Our two kids thought divorce was a fine idea, although they were concerned that it would make holidays a bit more complicated, what with an extra venue to squeeze into their busy schedules. My god...

The sudden upswing of domestic hostility left me somewhat preoccupied on the home front, and record-setting snowfalls kept roads only quasi-passable most of January. I wasn't able to get to Peaceful Pastures, but Stephanie was a regular iWhatchamacallit chatterbox, keeping me updated on events. Actually, there were no significant events, just life passing by.

I stared point blank at a different future, but one seemingly filled with new promise. Retirement was not far in the distance. And unless America came up with an enormous case of collective amnesia, it would be a cold day in hell before it elected another right-wing chick to national office, which meant what was left of my entitlements was safe. As for hell freezing over, well, not in the cards. Arctic regions were melting at increasing rates. All that extra water had to go somewhere, and the Midwest, the great American drain, was as good a place as any. Record flooding was being predicted for the spring.

I was set for my twilight years. All I had to do was figure out how to spend my free time.

I was finally able to get to Burgfort in early February. I stopped in at Jake's garage before checking up on Rotz and Steph. The streets were clear and dry, and I got my first lesson in cycle riding. Jake had a little electric scooter, no gears or clutch, and he showed me the rudiments of driving one of them – accelerator and front brake in right hand, rear break under right foot. He gave me a spare helmet and away I went, around the block. I was surprised at how easy it was, how much fun, like a bicycle, only less wear and tear on the knees. The wind was cold – I didn't care, I wasn't going very fast. When I got back to the shop, Jake showed me how to get moving from a dead start whether I was turning right or left or just going straight. I took off around town, around the Castle University campus; it was exhilarating.

When I was done, I thanked Jake and offered to pay him for the lesson. He wouldn't hear of it. I checked in on Rotz's bike. The machine mesmerized me. I was drawn to it. I sat on it for the first time – it was totally comfortable and plush, like an easy chair. I pulled it up from the kick stand to vertical. It was heavy. Jake stood behind me, ready to catch it if it fell. "Know how much this hog is worth?" he asked. I hadn't a clue. So he told me. I didn't believe him. I looked it up later on a Harley site. It was worth what he'd said and then some, a very expensive piece of machinery, a small fortune.

I went to Peaceful Pastures, to Steph and Rotz's room. It was already decorated for Valentine's Day. Hearts and flowers, pink stuff everywhere.

I didn't feel like hearing stories, and Rotz didn't seem to want to tell any. Instead, we spoke of my divorce.

"Don't get trampled," he advised.

"Bleed the bitch," Stephanie chimed in.

I assured them I was taking care of business, that I had received much advice from friends and business associates, even from the occasional attorney acquaintance. I felt I had things in hand and would come out ahead in the deal.

The three of us drove over to the Hawk, where Joe set us up immediately with beer. We sat at Rotz's booth and talked. They were planning a trip. I offered to pay, but Supreme had it covered. I was concerned about travel for him. What about the little cart that was mandatory if he were to get around? I was assured such things could be rented anywhere.

Shortly before Valentine's Day, I drove them to the city where they got on a plane to California to visit Rotz's daughter, so Steph could meet her.

I drove back home from the airport after seeing them off. It was eerily quiet. I reflected on the amazement I'd watched grow around me. A mere eight months ago, I'd been encumbered by two senior citizens who were finished, decrepit, with minds dulled by time and tide. They had been consigned to the refuse heap of an assisted living community.

Love had resuscitated both. Its power could not be underestimated.

When I had first met Rotz, he'd been embittered, irascible, ornery, an angry old man. Well, he had also been alone, with no real reason to go on. He had mellowed though, was a different person.

Cotta had sustained him, was maybe the only thing that had addressed his pain during that passage. Having become a cultural outcast, it followed he would embrace the most counter-culture piece of his life, that great, insane House and the championship football season it somehow managed to nurture and enable. He had retreated to that, and it had seen him through.

I started drinking that afternoon, rum, trying to put things into perspective. I envied the contentment Rotz had found in Stephanie and she in him. I realized how angry I myself was, had become. I had a wife, soon to be ex, who was ungrateful. I had kids who had forgotten about me. I was by myself. All I had done for this world, and there was nothing around me but uncaring SOBs. All the work I'd put in... Forget last month or even last year, nobody even remembered last week anymore. What have you done for me yesterday afternoon?

I didn't matter. I was sure my kids were monitoring me in their way, wondering when they'd have to check me into to some nursing home where I could be forgotten. Had the world always been this selfish, this destabilized, this cruel? Or was I just beginning to notice? I had been so happy, had thought the divorce would change things.

Now I had no future, that I could see...

The only positive in my life was on a plane to California. I smiled as I pictured my little charges, flying first class no less, heading for warm beaches and palm trees and sunshine.

Then I remembered I was a Cotta man now. The world was not going to toss me on the ash heap, not just yet. Fuck 'em. They could all take a fuckin' hike.

Embraced by that reassuring thought, I fell fast asleep on the only couch Deirdre had left me.

Steph kept me current on the great holiday voyage with little vid clips. Their luxury hotel was just ducky. Rotz was sunning on the veranda. The Jacuzzi worked wonders. The weather was fabulous.

The next Monday, I showed up for work to discover they needed volunteers for early retirement and were offering incentives. My new, Rotz-enhanced vision allowed me to see that my workplace had become a complete and utter wasteland. I ran my entire financial situation through an iGazornenplatt twice to make sure all was well there. I'd been paying into workman's comp and Social Security all my life. I had life insurance policies ready to mature. Now I'd get those payments in addition to early retirement bonuses and my pension. It was conceivable that I'd be making far more money by not working than working. I was completely set for life. I stepped right up and told 'em I'd take it. *Oh beautiful for spacious skies...*

Steph and Rotz stayed away an extra week because they decided to slip out to Hawaii. By the time they returned, I was closing down my little cubicle at *Medical Consultants R Us.* I met them at the airport, and we all caught up during the ride to Burgfort. They looked marvelous, tanned, 10 or 20 years younger, rejuvenated. It didn't seem right that I was taking them back to an assisted living center. They seemed very self-sufficient. They were happy to go home, however. And if it ain't broke, don't fix it.

After dropping them off, I stopped in at Jake's, got another lesson in power cyclery, and let the van drive me back to the city.

I followed a tip from Jake and went to a place in the suburbs to order a custom Harley helmet.

Having eschewed haircuts all this time, I decided to stop shaving as well.

21. The Battle of Cotta

The divorce went final before the vernal equinox. It was warming rapidly that spring. I drove to Burgfort to get another cycle lesson, by way of celebrating. It was all I could think of to do. I'd been given my perfunctory retirement party at the office. Whatta crocka shit that was. I had to sit and listen to platitudes coming from executives who didn't even know me. I was suddenly without wife and work. I'd thought I'd be happy, but I was panicking. What had looked so good a mere month ago had suddenly become a desperate passage. Nobody wanted or needed me. I was alone. Washed up. Finished.

Jake took the Harley out and gave me a ride on it for the first time. I sat behind him as he headed for an open road bathed in sunshine. Christ, what a rush! All that power rumbling under my ass, the absolute noise of the engine. I was determined to take it out on my own as soon as I could.

I picked up Rotz at PP, and while driving over to Joe's Hawk he filled me in on the great voyage west, although to hear his version of events about the only thing that happened was crazed sex in exotic locales. He still had that old one-track mind.

We settled in at his table. Joe brought us a round, then went back to his cleaning. The Hawk was the most immaculate tavern I'd ever seen, but Joe was nonetheless always frittering.

I mentioned that the snow was melting quickly. Rotz took a sip of beer, nodded, and got that far-away look in his eyes as he stared over my shoulder, out the window to the empty campus beyond.

"Wanna hear a Cotta story?" he asked.

"Sure," I said.

"It was spring," he began, "about this time of year. We had a German tradition at Einfahrt called *Ausflug*. We got an *Ausflug* once a semester, autumn and spring. What it meant was students got to call off classes and have a free day."

"That was nice," I said without much enthusiasm.

"Yeah, it was great. But, to put it into practice was never easy. There was this sequence of events to traverse. Somehow, a major portion of the student body had to agree on when it would be. And there was no overriding executive body to help."

"How was it decided?"

"Well, it was tricky. You had to politic. Students would walk around the campus at night and every once in a while scream 'Ausflug' and see if anyone else screamed it back. And we had to keep an eye on the weather forecasts, because we didn't want to have it on a crummy day. And we couldn't have it on a Monday or Friday, for obvious reasons. So this tension would be set up. And finally, a small group of students would go around one night trying to fire up enough students to get *Ausflug* called. If you couldn't get enough students, well, you packed it in and tried again another night. There was always the danger that you'd be so sure you'd have *Ausflug* that you'd stay up drinking, and then they wouldn't have it, and you were fucked. In fact, even if you did get it called, a lotta people spent the morning dealing with hangovers and slept that afternoon, instead of swimming and sunning and playing Frisbee golf and shit."

"There musta been lots of arguments. I mean, it sounds contentious."

"Actually, it wasn't so bad. If the drive for *Ausflug* made it through a night, then a crowd of students would gather at the heart of the campus at daybreak. At that juncture, you could see and feel if it was gonna happen. And this great chant would go up, 'Ausflug, Ausflug.' Very loud, maybe 300, 400 students."

"Tribal," I noted.

"A jovial mob," he recalled with a smile. "Well then, tradition dictated that those students had to find the Student Body President. At this point, the crowd would grow. Once they found the SBP, they had to take him from his hiding place and walk over to the College President's residence, which was on campus. The College President would come out his front door, and the SBP would formally request *Ausflug* and the CP would grant it, of course, assuming there was a crowd of students in support, and everybody would go over to the caf for breakfast and then take the day off."

"Sounds interesting."

"Yeah, something to do to break the monotony of classes. Now, this particular spring, the SBP turned out to be Baity-ro's friend, Ron Ball, who was a darned good poet by the way. He went on to a long career writing training manuals for the Defense Department, which is what happens to poets in America." He thought for a second. "Wonder if he ever learned Chinese... Anyway, they worked it out that Ball would hide in Cotta."

"What could possibly go wrong with that?" I was being facetious.

"Cotta could go wrong with that," Rotz laughed. "We took a brief look at the basic tradition and saw it with new, somewhat bloodshot, eyes. That little 'find the SBP' thing seemed a bit silly to us. We didn't think that sounded like much fun. We convened a quick House meeting and decided to put our own spin on it."

"Oh boy," I said.

"Yes, *Ausflug* was in the air that fateful spring afternoon, my friend, and Ball came over to the House early evening. The boys decided to defend Cotta like some fortress, see if the students could break in and get him out."

"Naturally. Even I woulda thoughta that."

He sniffed. "We had a council of war, plans were drawn up on paper. Since we'd already started drinking heavily, they were hastily scrawled plans, as if struck by some elementary school students, but basically the windows and doors were to be manned as best we could defend them.

Since there were as many downstairs windows and doors as there were guys, this would be a challenge.

"We strung one of those wire picket fences around the House, not on the lawn, but around the structure itself, across the first-floor windows. Boards were nailed inside the two doors, across them front and back. The main instrument of defense, other than big linemen, was to be water. Water hoses were screwed onto the outdoor faucets and brought into the house through windows that were opened just a crack, hundreds of water balloons were lovingly filled. Oh, and there was a bucket to collect pee in the upstairs can. No one could piss anyplace but that bucket."

"Oh Rotz," I said with some disappointment.

"Well, it was Cotta."

"You didn't shit in it, did you?"

"No, that probably would've weirded even us out."

"Thank heaven for small favors."

"Hey, we coulda planned dangerous stuff, but we didn't wanna hurt anybody. We just wanted to have some fun, not send people to the hospital. In any event, nobody got much sleep that night. We figured the students would show up around 4 or 5 AM. And we had a lotta work to do getting the House ready for battle. Beer came into the place in cases. Meanwhile, cries of *Ausflug* continued to fill the air over on campus."

"Sounds bucolic and romantic," I reflected.

Rotz laughed. "It would be a splashy ending to a long year," he said. "And less than 20 guys were going to have to keep 400 students out of Cotta House. And remember, there were lots more football players and wrestlers outside than in. We knew it wouldn't be a cakewalk.

"So the sky in the east started to lighten." He pointed out the window. "Cotta was located back over there, across the street from the rear of the home stands and the football field press box. From our upstairs windows there was an unobstructed view of campus. In the gloom we could see the students gathering, and we could hear them chanting, 'Ausflug, Ausflug.' We manned our stations and waited. We watched the crowd walk over to The Fertile Crescent, and when the girls exited those dorms, the group became a quorum surely. So it was on. Then they had to find Ball. Well,

Ball's hiding place was a poorly-kept secret. We watched them walk north, across the street from the football field, to the upperclassmen's living quarters, the Manors. Those emptied out and the herd swelled, a festive and mirthful group of college students heading inexorably for Cotta House."

"Golly, that just sounds terrific," I said dryly.

"The football field extended to our left as you looked out the front of Cotta," he continued, ignoring me, "and the students walked down the avenue beyond the north end goal posts, took a left, and headed up the street to the House just as the sun was about to break the horizon."

"Seems so pastoral." I smiled.

"Well, it was," he agreed. "We had turned all our lights off, and we kept away from the windows. Nobody said a thing. Everything in Cotta was totally dark and quiet. And the crowd came walking up the street, all happy and dancing and chanting and like that. And then a strange thing happened."

I wondered what could possibly be considered strange by a Cotta man. "What?" I asked.

"What what?"

"What was strange?"

"Oh. Well, Cotta was easily the best House on campus, the most prestigious."

"How was that even remotely possible?" I wondered aloud.

Rotz pursed his lips in thought. "Physical power is not to be sneezed at, and there was a lotta beef in that place. Plus, we had all the fun. We were all very good-looking," he smiled, "and we were nice guys."

"You were?"

"Well, yeah. I mean, the Cotta ethic, such as it was, morphed out in several directions, a few of which weren't especially salutary. But by and large, our hearts were in the right place. We turned out OK. We were unpredictable, maybe that was it."

"You were unbelievably gross."

"Yeah, but that's a plus for kids."

"You were incorrigibly profane."

"Also a plus."

"You were dangerous."

"Marv, those are all *plus*es. Anyway, there was that prevailing aura – you didn't fuck with Cotta. And to boot, we had guests in the House all the time, ladies, you know."

"For sex?"

"Marv, must you always try to cheapen everything?" He got that playful look on his face, with his infectious grin. "You know, I can't ever recall anybody ever getting laid in the house proper. There was a bunk bed in every room, so with a guy above or below you, well, a deal breaker. It was too public."

"You poor babies," I said without much conviction.

"Well, back then we considered a *mènage a trois* perverse, more's the pity. And there were friendly motels all over the county, no questions asked. We did have lotsa parties though. The basement barroom was way cool. Our spring woodsies were the social events of the year. So, other students knew about the place, had heard the stories, some knew the layout of the House. Most of us usually had girl friends, after all, the girls were dropping by all the time. And our status had soared after that championship season. We were gentle, somewhat screwball, giants. It was a sexy place, just no sex." His mind drifted off, lost in the digression.

I brought him back to the story. "You said the students did something strange..."

"Oh yeah, well, when they got to the corner by the House, in the shadow of the football stands, they suddenly stopped. They stopped everything. Stopped walking, stopped chanting, stopped laughing. I guess the place looked slightly foreboding, sitting there so quiet in the dawn."

"Well, it was capable of anything, after all."

"Yes it was. And that probably had occurred to them, some flash of insight as the vibe of the place seeped out beyond the confines of the structure itself. We kept totally quiet, watched them only by peeking out from the corners of windows. They held some kind of meeting. And finally, one brave soul was sent to knock on our front door, polite like. I thought that was a nice touch. So he walks up and knocks, then quickly runs back to the safety of the crowd. And we ignore it. Nothing. Just silence. You had to admire our discipline."

I was starting to laugh again.

"The crowd waited a while, and put its collective head together, and finally started chanting, 'We want Ball, we want Ball,' and so on… and that didn't work either. Meanwhile, inside, we were getting ready. And a signal was given, and Port City, the designated communicator for the morning, sticks his head out of the front gable on the roof, the one that came off the attic.

"He constituted a disturbing presence, wearing as he was his black plastic Nazi helmet. I looked up out of my window to see his pugnacious profile, jaw thrust forward, framed in a perfect, pale blue, cloudless morning sky.

"The crowd gasped, shrank back. He waited until it went totally quiet. Then he screamed down to them, 'You *fucking* want Ball, you *fucking* come and get him!'"

"Holy shit," I said.

"Yeah, no one had told him quite what words to use, but as we would reminisce back over the decades at reunions, we came to judge those as just about the perfect way to express it."

"Well naturally."

"And the coeds instinctively recoiled, moving away to watch while the guys eventually slowly advanced on the perimeter. We let loose the first volley of water balloons, and the assault on Cotta was joined. Everybody seemed to get the rules, or the complete absence thereof, right away. I mean, there were no speeches, no delineations. In no time at all, we heard the pounding on the front porch as burly shoulders slammed against the door and shook the boards we'd nailed up to secure it. Then they came at the back door. There was the sound of breaking glass, the windows…

"The water hoses were fired up. The bucket of piss was slung from the roof over the porch and scored a direct hit on some kid bent over and running to the House. He was wearing a ski parka which I'm sure got washed forthwith. As near as we can figure, they broke through the back door first. And since there was already water all over the ground floor from the hoses, it was slippery, and the bigger guys bent to the task of throwing the intruders out the door from whence they had come. It quickly descended into a mass free-for-all. It was like, well, like a ballet.

"One guy managed to make it to the steps leading upstairs. There was a window on the landing about half way up. Rory was descending and met him and indicated to the kid that if he didn't jump out the window on his own, he'd be thrown out. He chose wisely and jettisoned himself, there being a better chance at a safer landing I guess. But he wasn't fast enough, quite, and McRory was urgently needed elsewhere, apparently, and so hit the kid's hands as he hung nervously from the sill, providing much-needed motivation. It was kind of a long fall."

"I got a question," I interrupted.

"Shoot."

"Where was the Student Body President? He couldn't possibly have appreciated this."

"Well, craven politician that he was, he got cold feet early. He watched the conflagration from the relative safety of the second floor. And the sounds alone were compelling, very loud. All that yelling and cursing and sloshing from downstairs. He was laughing his ass off on the one hand and worrying about how the hell he was gonna get out of the muddle on the other. The prospect of him getting blamed was troubling to him. We were all on unfamiliar turf here. No one had ever done this on *Ausflug*, and nobody ever did it again, by the way. Sequels never seem to work well. This was unique.

"Anyhow, some little wrestler smashed through the front door, where Dimro unceremoniously punched him in the nose, discouraging him. But they kept pouring in the back door. We were throwing water balloons from upstairs while guys wrestled in water downstairs, and the invaders kept coming. The coeds were laughing and cheering, watching in stunned amazement."

"How did it end?" I asked innocently.

"Ball finally got totally cold feet and called a halt, just about the right time, I think. He came forth out the back door and walked around front, surrounded by triumphant Teuton warriors, a consort of guys who looked like they'd gone swimming in their clothing. An enormous cheer went up from the crowd. I can't imagine what the whole scene must've looked like from their vantage point."

"Anybody get hurt?"

"Naw, some bumps and bruises, but amazingly, just good clean fun."

"That's very hard to believe." I raised my hand and Joe brought us a fresh round and some fries. "Didn't anybody call the cops? Where were the campus police?"

"There was only one campus cop that I knew of, and he surely was asleep at that early hour. The Burgfort officers, same, probably. And people didn't call authorities at the drop of a hat back then, like all these wusses do now. This was before the 911 call system was even dreamt of, you know."

"Surely someone complained," I insisted.

"Not that I know of. We took the worst of it. Every stick of furniture in the living room was smashed, including the Pepper table."

"Geez, I'm sorry Supreme," I managed with mock concern.

"Well, they were barbarians," he shot back, "common ruffians. No respect." He softened. "But we were not ones to hold a grudge. We went over to eat breakfast with everybody while the water dripped out of the House. It was pouring into the basement, but there were drains down there. We sang the Cotta song at the top of our lungs as we walked to the caf. The student body was in an especially festive mood when we got there. Most agreed it was the perfect thing to diffuse the tension building up in early spring, midterms and all."

I shook my head in disbelief. "Nobody from the administration gave you hell? No formal reprimands, no fines? No consequences?"

"None that any of us can recall."

"What about a school newspaper, did you have one of those?"

"Yeah, *The Einfahrt Trumpet.* We called it *The Strumpet.*"

"Well I'm sure you did. Did they comment?"

"At the height of the battle, a *Strumpet* photographer yelled up to my second floor window to ask if he could approach the House and get a few pictures of the crowd attacking. Potz and I told him sure and he backed up to the House, his camera to his eye, snapping away I would suppose. When he got close enough, we dumped a bucket of water on him, direct hit."

"So much for currying favor with the Fourth Estate."

"Yeah, I hope his camera survived." Rotz laughed. "And yes, there was a short article, boilerplate as I recall, a couple of pictures, front page. They didn't quite know what to make of it."

"This didn't rise to the level of newsworthy?"

"Barely."

"It just slid on by?" I was incredulous.

"Just another day in the life. Oh, there was that editorial. I think there's still a copy of it around here somewhere."

He called to Joe and asked about it. Joe walked over to a nondescript corner of a distant wall, lifted a small frame off it, was dusting it with a bar rag as he brought it and handed to me. Behind cloudy glass was a yellowed piece of newsprint. I read the headline aloud, "Poor Taste Is Displayed."

"That would be us," Rotz said. Joe laughed and returned to his bar to fiddle.

"Here it is, by god," I said, "One victim was forced from a window one and a half stories from the ground."

"Told you," Rotz said.

I continued reading to him. "SBP Ball attempted to halt the proceedings as soon as the trouble began. His efforts were too little and too late, however, and the unfortunate incident occurred anyway."

"Oh right," Rotz opined with a big guffaw. "That was his story after the fact. He was up to his ears in it. Although, I'm not certain he really knew what he was getting himself into. None of us did."

I went on, "The real blame lies with the persons in the house who used their physical strength in an unwise manner. The Trumpet hopes that the Cotta men realize that their actions were a mistake and could have resulted in serious injury."

"Not exactly F. Scott Fitzgerald at the pen there," Supreme whiffed dismissively.

"Did you meditate on the errors of your ways?" I asked.

He rolled his eyes and pointed to the article. "This was music to our ears."

"Rotz, lemme ask you something," I said.

"OK."

"Why doesn't this stuff go on today? What happened to all this campus insanity?"

He thought for a moment. "It still goes on, sort of. But if you recall, end of the century, things got out of hand with the initiations and parties and shit. Students were dying from alcohol poisoning and like that. Meanwhile, the cost of higher education was skyrocketing. You had kids who were working their entire adult lives to pay off college loans. Parents insisted that if they were going to spend so much money, at the very least their children should not turn up dead on campus, which I think was a reasonable expectation. And so here came all these rules, and higher education became a more serious place."

He paused and there was an afterthought. "Then, about the same time, this wave of political correctness swept through, all these fucking do-gooders trying to tell everyone how to behave, this narrow, tight-ass confinement to total intellectual sterility. That's when the American office began going to hell. No more dirty jokes around the water cooler. No more admiring some secretary's tits aloud. No *secretaries*, for that matter. Life went out of the workplace, and humanity with it. The finger-pointers were triumphant, everybody was jumping everybody else's shit. It was a disaster. Everything got boring and people got afraid."

I never ceased to be amazed at the extent of Rotzinger's purview. I wondered if there were any subjects he hadn't thought about at some time or another. Of course, he'd had lots of time to think.

"Have you heard about what's been happening to me?" I asked him.

"Steph keeps me appraised," he replied, "a time of changeover."

I laughed, "You could call it that."

"I just did," he noted.

"Well, you know, for most of my adult life, things have been in place – home, family, profession, salary, stuff like that."

"Yes, well?"

"It's all gone. Last month, I had a wife and a job. I was important. I mattered. Now…" I threw up my hands in futility.

"Now it's all fucked," he said simply. "Welcome to your golden years." He spread his arms expansively.

"But I don't matter anymore," I protested.

"Sure you do," he consoled. "You just matter in a different way to different people. See, Marv, when one door closes, another opens. I think that's like Buddhist or something. You just have to look for the open door instead of fixating on what has closed."

"It pisses me off."

"It's life. Life still pisses me off after all this time. It always will, I reckon."

"Well, I can't even go visit my kids. I'm just in the way."

"Then go somewhere else."

"Where?"

"I dunno. Look on the bright side. You have money and free time. You have no obligations. You're set for the duration."

"Nobody needs me."

He took a pull of beer, lifted his glass to me, grinned, and said, "Freedom's just another word for nothin' left to lose."

I let him pick up the tab. I didn't mention a tip.

22. To Everything, There Is a Season

April brought warm weather early. The thaw was quick and the flooding in the Dakotas, massive. Fargo was under water again, as well as what was left of Minot. I was lolling around, getting depressed, watching the world by myself in my house, when my custom helmet was delivered. I decided to take it to Burgfort and learn how to ride Rotz's Harley.

The motel was old and Spartan but squeaky clean. It was also cheap. I booked a room for a week and drove over to Jake's garage. He started by showing me how to work the helmet. It had a two-way talk system in addition to the radio, which was satellite. A computer could pull up all sorts of specific information from the Internets by voice command. Audio GPS of course. Everything voice-activated, hands free. I could do my banking on it, pay bills and whatnot, all I had to do was summon up my finance bot and talk with it. Really simple. Of course, most of that had been automatic for a long time. Money, or whatever it was, simply flowed around silently in the background.

Jake mounted the bike and I got on the back and he drove us over to a big, empty Castle University parking lot. He told me to get in the driver's saddle, then he got on the buddy seat. I was scared but game. I'd never learned to shift anything manually, since all my cars had been automatic transmission jobs. The first couple of tries with the clutch, I killed it. One time it would have fallen over had not Jake been in back helping me keep it vertical. Surprisingly, when centered it wasn't that heavy for such a big bike. It was delicate, sensitive, had balance.

On my fourth try I got it going straight. I didn't have to turn or shift out of first, all he wanted me to do was get from one side of the lot to the other, then disengage the clutch, brake it, and put my feet on the pavement. I somehow managed. Together, while it idled, we turned the bike around with our feet, and I drove it straight to the other side. We did this simple exercise for nearly an hour. Then Jake drove us back to his shop.

"Sleep on it," he said. "Come back tomorrow. You'll be better, trust me."

I went over to The Hawk for lunch – Joe made the best burgers in the world – then to Peaceful Pastures. Rotz and Steph were napping, so I left word I'd be back to take them to dinner and went and charged the van. Then I drove out of town and around the countryside, relaxing and sight-seeing. I had a lot of trouble getting used to the idea that I had nothing in particular to do. I chanced upon a roadside park and stopped. I took out a small blanket, laid it under a tree by the Maple River, and fell asleep listening to the water lapping against the banks. I awoke and thought for a bit. Perhaps I could go on a camping trip. I hadn't done that in a long time, decades it seemed, not since the kids were young. Camping wasn't much fun alone though.

I returned to the motel, showered and dressed, and picked up my two buddies at Peaceful Pastures. I helped Rotz walk to the van with his cane. We visited one of his favorite restaurants in a nearby city and ate well. The talk was small and that was a relief. Routine was setting in. This trio was now an established ritual, nothing new or special about it. It was simply another day. Both of them looked great, were doing great. I got them back to PP early and headed to Joe's for a nightcap. There was something in the predictability of it all that was comforting.

Next day, I drove the Harley by myself for the first time, straight across the parking lot. It still felt totally foreign, but I was heartened by my progress. I went back and forth, over and over. I still had no fucking idea what I was doing on a chopper, but such was what life had handed me. I couldn't think of anything else to do with the time. The bike was powerful – as were Rotz and Steph, in their way. Power, however random, seemed to be gathering around me. The two of them were acting like a couple, sparring around, griping at each other. They were inspiring. I started looking at women again, first time in decades really.

As the week progressed, Jake moved me out into small side streets. He had patience, that was for sure. He told me that over the years he'd taught lots of people to ride, never lost one.

By the end of the week, I was driving the Harley around the block by myself in first gear. It was beginning to feel somewhat comfortable. I still had to concentrate a lot though. It was work. Jake said the big bikes were made for the open road. They were easy at 80 miles an hour. City driving was hard, but I had to learn city riding first. Sort of like taking off and landing a plane .

At week's end I said good-bye to everyone and rode back home in the van. I spent the trip trying to think of anything I really had wanted to do for the past thirty years and had never quite gotten around to. I drew a complete blank on that one.

Somewhere deep inside, I knew if I didn't find something to fill the empty spaces, I'd curl up on my couch and die. I'd cultivated no hobbies, had few interests. I decided to buy some weights and see if I liked working out. Lord knows, there was lots of room in my basement. I wanted to shed a few pounds and feel healthier. I wanted to eat better, so I looked into that too. And I started dictating Rotz's stories into my iCowabunga, which converted them immediately to type. I didn't want to forget them.

It was a beginning.

In late April I went back to Burgfort for another week and took more Harley lessons. I again offered to pay Jake but he again refused. Said he owed it to Rotz. He taught me how to shift, which turned out to be easier than I had expected. We got it out on the highway – I drove a Harley on the highway, baby, 50 miles an hour, with Jake behind me on the buddy seat, talking helmet to helmet. I had nice meals with Steph and Rotz. We chatted about stuff that didn't matter in the least.

I returned to the city and ate well, slept well, and worked out. I was starting to feel better, slowly adjusting. And everything was just fine. Until I got the urgent vid from Steph... "Come quick, Marv, it's Rotz."

I talked with her as the van drove to Burgfort. He was in intensive care, facing a complete circulatory system collapse. His heart had simply given out. His daughter was on her way, would be there tomorrow night.

The hospital wasn't far from Peaceful Pastures. Steph met me there. The last time I'd seen her this sad was when Mom died.

The ICU was dimly lit. Rotz was sleeping peacefully as they ushered us in. He was surrounded by machines, little glowing lights and beepy things. He was hooked up to tubes and wires. We'd been warned to keep the peace, no stress. We sat side-by-side on chairs, against the wall in the gloom. I wasn't sure what we were waiting for, exactly. The doctor couldn't really tell us anything. He said there were no treatment options remaining; they'd been doing everything possible for years. They could only try to keep him comfortable and hope his body would pull him through.

It was about the last place I wanted to be. Yet I recalled that Rotz had known this was coming. He was resigned to it, even at ease with it.

He awoke at suppertime. They propped him up and he managed to eat a bit. He didn't say much, smiled weakly at us. We asked if we could bring him anything. No, he was fine. The staff guided us out so he could get a good night's sleep.

Steph and I went to The Hawk for dinner, but neither of us could eat. We sipped wine, brought Joe up to date. He said he'd visit the next day. I wondered if there would be a next day.

Steph looked at me across the table, her chin in her hands. She had obviously been crying a lot. I couldn't think of anything to say or do. It didn't feel good at all. Rotz had looked so delicate. She said he'd just collapsed in their room, fell to the floor coming back from the bathroom. She'd caught him, sort of. His head hadn't hit the carpet. They'd taken him straight to the hospital, no screwing around. She told me no one had to tell her it was serious. Everyone knew instantly.

I stayed with her until she was ready to go to bed. They'd contact her if there were any developments in the night. They'd wake her and she'd call me. She wanted to sleep in her room, so I dropped her off at the Complex and went back to the motel. I didn't sleep much.

The next morning, early, I picked her up and we returned to the hospital to keep a vigil in the waiting room. There had been no real change in Rotz's condition overnight. He was no worse, but no better either. One is totally helpless at such times. We went in to be with him when they let us, and came out when they told us. Rotz was alert, just very infirm.

Steph and I talked to each other as best we could in the waiting room. Things had been going so well. That's what neither of us could comprehend. Things had been going so well, why now? when the two of them had finally found something to live for. Why death now?

I didn't know much about Supreme's life, other than the Cotta years. I tried to picture him walking around the college, on the football field. He would have been so vital. And all that craziness… I presumed he'd lived his entire life like that, had gotten everything he could out of it, right down to the marrow. He'd been everything he was supposed to be, had taken things as they came, made the best of it all, had never given in. He had moved from era to era, role to role, with aplomb.

Late that afternoon, two doctors asked us to come to the waiting room. They advised us we should say good-bye to Rotzinger. They were losing him – we were losing him.

We walked carefully to his bedside, and he turned his head slowly and recognized us. Almost imperceptibly, he brightened. Steph held back, and he talked to me first. His speech was labored. "Jake says you're riding the bike."

"Yes," I told him, "not well, but there's progress."

I held his hand, the first time I'd done that since we'd met. It was cold and lifeless. A lump rose in my throat. "How are you?" I asked softly.

"About done," he whispered.

I was in tears. "Please stay," I pleaded.

He waited for the strength to speak. "Outta my hands. I'll be fine."

I know he trusted that. All that religion stuff from his youth, belief systems. I could barely talk. He asked me to take care of Steph for him, and I told him not to worry about that. Of course I would.

"You're the last Cotta man now," he said, his eyes slowly closing, and I felt him weakly squeeze my hand. I put my cheek to his head and hugged it.

"Thanks for all you did for me... and Steph," I said.

He replied almost inaudibly, "Thanks to you Marv... vaya con dios, muchacho... I love you brother... Cotta forever..."

I walked away in a daze, filled with frustration. I watched Steph approach him and sit next to him on his bed. They held hands, talking in whispers for quite a while, until a doctor and nurse slowly appeared from out of the shadows. They'd been monitoring the machines. They said it was time.

And Rotz closed his eyes. I stood nearby. He said nothing, simply passed on with dignity. The doctor examined him, waiting for a long while, then finally asked that the machines be disconnected. Nurses turned them off, took them from his body, and rolled them out of the room, one by one.

Steph and I were alone with him. I moved her chair to the bed. She sat with him in perfect quiet, her hand on his arm.

At last she stood and walked over to me. We held each other and wept. A nurse returned to fetch one last machine and gently said, "We'll be back in a while, take your time. Let us know when you're finished."

Then it was quiet again.

Steph finally broke the silence. "He treated me like a lady, Marv, a lady, always," she sobbed. "He was the best I ever had."

"Yes," was all I could think to say. I was sure he was. He was the father I'd never had – the only mentor I'd ever known.

"He was the only man I ever loved," she went on. "Do you know that he led his high school basketball team to the State championship? They won it all. He averaged 20 points a game."

I told her I hadn't known that.

"He was a true champion, my champion," she whispered, then was silent.

Tears rolled down my cheeks. Stephanie fell into more whimpers, poor thing, and looked up at me, smiling through her sorrow, trying to be brave, whispering almost to herself, "He had the most enormous dick."

23. THE RETURN

I went back to the city to get some decent clothes for the funeral. Rotz's daughter arrived shortly after his death and finalized all arrangements. Auntie Stephanie stayed at Peaceful Pastures to help.

Rotz was buried next to his wife in the Burgfort countryside near the outskirts of town, the Lutheran cemetery. God forbid he should be buried anywhere near Papists. Jake was there, and Joe. Rotz's daughter and a preacher. Me and Steph. It was a sunny morning, warm and calm. After his impressive coffin was lowered into the ground, we went to the church he had once attended years prior and celebrated his life.

In listening, I was assured that Supreme had been blessed with many friends and colleagues. He was indeed an important person. He had come from a good family and had built another. But all those people had passed on or moved away, his brothers and sisters long since departed, their kids scattered, leaving only this little cluster of misfits to consider what he had meant in the great scheme of things.

When it came my turn to speak, I said he had made a considerable impact upon me, that he had changed my life, that losing him was like losing my best friend. This was the truth.

He had been a similar inspiration to others... a fine father and grandfather.

I had suggested to Steph prior to the service that she confine her remarks to his spiritual effect on her life and was greatly relieved when she did. She said he had found her and saved her, and I was certain this was true as well.

When the formal ceremonies were over, the little cluster of mourners retreated to Joe's Hawk for food and drink. It was an oddly appropriate place to remember Rotz in the ribald fullness of his ministry to us all. As the conversations began to gain strength, as story upon story was shared and laughter returned, I was struck by how giving he had, apparently, always been. And what a leader he was. A powerful spirit...

It was late in the afternoon before we were ready to stop remembering for a bit and get back to the real world. I knew I would be seeing Jake and Joe for the duration.

The next morning, I got on the Harley with Jake and drove it into the countryside. I had gained confidence in my ability to negotiate the hills and valleys of those rural two-lane blacktops. I dropped him off at his garage and went back out on my own. I drove around for hours, staring out the Mars-Age face-plate at the black, manicured fields, ready for planting. Somehow, the sun, although bright, wasn't a problem. The mirrored visor had been tempered – I could see out clearly, yet it acted like a large pair of sunglasses. Remarkable. Same technology as the folks who were living on the moon.

Passing motorists would stare with respect at the bike itself, the sheer iconoclastic beauty of it. I took it back to Jake's and we talked about getting it to my house in the city. He told me I was now a graduate of his motorcycle course. He said he could rent a small trailer one-way, and I could just haul it behind my van.

I left Steph at Peaceful Pastures and took the Harley home. I had plenty of space for it in the garage, since Deirdre had taken so much stuff with her.

I got a call from Steph a few days later. She had shown up in Rotz's will, was the beneficiary of a fund which provided her a monthly stipend to live on, comfortably, in perpetuity. She was shocked. It turned out Rotz was worth more than most had imagined. He had also set up a small foundation for Peaceful Pastures. His daughter got the bulk of his estate.

Steph said there were some things he'd left for me as well, a gift that was in the mail. A few days later, several large packages arrived. In them were Rotz's biker leathers – pants and jackets. And all his football and Cotta House memorabilia. There was even the little trophy he'd received for winning the Iowa State basketball championship, his team's MVP award, as well as the awards for his championship football season and his All-Conference selections. The Cotta pictures that had filled his room at PP were there too, all those young faces and crazy outfits.

I was deeply moved as I sifted through all this stuff. It was in mint condition, carefully packaged. Rotz had been a neat freak of considerable proportions. In remembering him at the memorial service, this had been duly noted. Everything in his life had been organized and cared for. His desk was always empty and tidy. All was dealt with smartly and efficiently, no matter what.

I tried on the leathers. They looked dated, what with the fringe and all, but the fit was just about right. I was hoping to trim down in the upcoming months – that would do it.

I arranged his stuff in one of the spare bedrooms, hung the pictures on its walls.

I exercised, studied diet technologies, and fiddled around on my iDevices. I rode Rotz's Harley out into the country, taking ever-longer trips. I became one with the machine. I still was sticking to surface roads and staying off freeways, but was working my way up to them. I missed Number One Supreme very much.

I used my contacts from my old job to score some of that synthetic marijuana shit that was the newest rage, just to try it out. It was awesome. One could snap out of the cloud instantly simply by wanting to, then sink back in if one chose. I was struck by how cheap it was. Totally harmless, they said. There was already a movement to legalize it. I used it to help channel Rotz's Sixties as I watched old movies on the 3D walk-through entertainment system I'd managed to save from the swath Deirdre cut out of our possessions.

About a month after the funeral, I got a call from Steph. She was having trouble living at Peaceful Pastures. Memories of Rotz were all around her. Could she come and live with me for a while?

Well, of course. I told her to start packing immediately. A few days later I drove the van to Burgfort to get her. I loaded up all the boxes that would fit. The few that remained we addressed to my home, asking the staff to mail them for me. No *problemo*.

Auntie Stephanie was in excellent health, her faculties sharp as a tack. I spent some time talking with a member of the Peaceful Pastures medical staff and was assured she was good to go. She took a few prescription meds regularly, pills, but she could take them anywhere. They considered her an amazement of sorts. Few people at PP ever went back home after arriving.

We checked her out and returned to the city.

She had her basement suite back. In a few days it was put together, good as before, maybe even better. It was great having her around. She was, as always, wonderful company. We cooked together, ate together, exercised together, watched movies together, walked and shopped together.

We ordered a helmet for her just like mine, only hers was to be air-brushed pink, with ultra-violet trim and sexy ladies in bikinis on it. In less than a month, it arrived. I showed her how all the technology in it worked, the communication system. We bought her some leather road clothing and a great pair of black, ass-kicking boots. We went riding, her on the rear buddy seat with her arms around me. My hair was now long enough to hang out from under my helmet and wave in the wind. We made a fine biker duo as we rolled through the countryside.

I was content for the first time since I could remember. Steph and I were set. It became easier considering things to do when she was around. Life began to open up for us again. We decided to take a trip to the West Coast on the bike, camping along the way. I talked with Jake and he assured me I could buy a small, two-wheel camper-trailer that came fitted out from the manufacturer with all the stuff we'd need – a tent, sleeping bags, air mattresses, cooking gear, the works. He also recommended an anti-theft gizmo for the Harley. I asked him to please order both.

Steph's entire life began to wrap around me. Although still a bundle of energy, she seemed to have no interest in going out on her own and making new friends. Apparently, Peaceful Pastures had gotten that little spasm of unimpeded partying out of her system. She became quite the homebody. She decorated and cleaned and bought furniture. She relaxed and rested as we studied maps and planned the great vacation. We'd go to all the places we'd always wanted to see but had never gotten to. The Grand Canyon, Yosemite, Vancouver, San Francisco...

She'd learned the Cotta song, as had I. We shared Supreme's stories. I had some she hadn't heard, she had some I hadn't heard. We laughed at them... they were like our secrets.

She was the most beautiful lady, the sweetest person. I loved her dearly, always had. We'd sit on the couch and watch movies together, sometimes far into the night, relaxing with wine and talking. We were completely on the same page.

And one evening, after I'd introduced her to the synthetic marijuana, she began to cuddle up to me, and was purring softly and nibbling on my neck, her breasts on my arm. For me, it produced a combination of great comfort and discomfort. I didn't like where it was going. I sought to disentangle from her.

"Please," I said.

"Oh Marvin, sweet, silly Marvin," she whispered coyly, in that sexy, little-girl voice of hers, like she'd whispered when I was a child, "you needn't worry about a thing."

"Why?" I wondered aloud.

"Marvin, look at me," she breathed.

I dared stare into her big blue eyes. She stared back, and took a deep breath.

"I was adopted," she said with a wink.

Silence, as that thunderbolt landed...

Well, what the hell, it had just plain been one of those years.

"I changed your diapers," she giggled. "You had the cutest little winkie…"

Oh yeah, that's right. I was reminded that this was Stephanie, after all, the irresistible, rebel force.

I couldn't believe what was about to happen…

24. Blank

25. And the Thunder Rolls

I awoke the next morning in my bed wrapped around Stephanie. We were both naked, save for her engagement ring. My first instinct was to recoil in horror. I rolled over on my back and was soon trying to straighten my head out as she lay on my right arm, purring beside me. Of course... it slowly began to make all the sense in the world, albeit furball.

Stephanie had never really fit into our family. She was the ugly duckling, a vivacious, petite, blue-eyed blonde floating around in a gene pool of large, plodding, stoic, brown-eyed brunettes. She didn't look like us or act like us. Not even close.

And I'd always wondered why I had been drawn to her as a young boy. Even back then, before I began to figure out sex, she had seemed inordinately, attractively fascinating. Actually, my childhood buddies had noticed it even before me, when they'd sleep over and Steph would be in charge. They would say that Aunt Stephanie was "righteous hot." They loved to spend the night at my place if they knew she'd be there babysitting. Even in her teens, she'd been stacked. And she didn't seem to mind if my little first-grade pals tackled her when she wasn't looking and wrestled with her on the living room carpet. Or just jumped on her when she was sitting and eating popcorn with us while we watched cartoons in our jammies, initiating what she called *Tickle-Rama*. In fact, she would laugh and writhe and scream with delight as they crawled all over her. Cheap feels, as it turns out, are instinctive, not some carefully devised adolescent stratagem. She always was a lotta fun.

I lay there looking at the ceiling, musing, and my head gradually became less scattered. I had even secretly wondered sometimes when I got older if in fact Steph had been adopted, because she and Mom were so different. After Steph had turned 18, she stayed well away from my grandparents, just kind of flew the coop.

My thoughts were interrupted when she woke up, yawned, and stretched luxuriously. Then she cuddled up against me. I asked her about the adoption and she explained it, filled in the missing pieces. Shortly after mom was born, my grandparents had wanted a sibling for her. They had tried and tried to no avail. So they decided on adoption, which took a while. This was why Steph was over 10 years younger than Mom and why that relationship was a bit rocky. By the time Steph arrived on the scene, Mom had gotten to enjoy being an only child and resented the attention lavished on this new baby sister.

My grandparents had been old school, if not old world, and were insecure about their inability to produce another child. So grandma had gone away for quite a while. Steph seemed to recall hearing somewhere that she'd gone to a sister's, to preserve the appearance that she'd been pregnant and Steph was one of their own. They had been that dysfunctional.

While both Mom and Steph might have had their suspicions, Mom hadn't been told Steph was adopted until after she'd gotten married, in large part because Steph was such a discipline problem. My grandparents figured that if she knew she'd been adopted, she'd be completely impossible to control. They didn't tell Steph until after she'd dropped out of college, about the same time they washed their hands of her. And because she was furious with her birth parents when she found out for certain what they'd done to her, she never sought to look for them. Apparently, no one had ever come looking for her either, poor thing.

My grandparents left her next to nothing in their will. Mom had gotten everything, leaving Steph to fend for herself. Mom, to her everlasting credit, took her in whenever she needed help. And took

Steph's secret to her grave. Which is how Auntie S had wound up with Deirdre and me. It all wove together, cleared up this big mystery that had been floating through my transom on and off my entire life.

Steph had always been afraid to tell me for fear I'd reject her, throw her out if I discovered she wasn't a blood relation. That made sense too. She was a rolling stone, a will-o'-the-wisp, a gypsy. She hadn't ever had much in the way of true financial stability.

It was a great load off my shoulders. The fantasies I'd had about Steph ever since I was a kid had intensified after that bizarre shower encounter, and I was always disturbed by those desires. I mean, it was weird having this *thing* for my aunt. I'd more or less put the concerns to rest when I reached adulthood. Obviously, happily as it turned out, they'd never quite died.

Auntie Stephanie was indeed everything Rotz had said she was, and then some.

Sufficed to say, the house took on an entirely different dynamic.

I had always loved Steph. I always would. No *problemo...*

She thought my beard was sexy.

And one mild afternoon in June, I went to a nearby Harley dealership to pick up my camper/trailer. They showed me how it all worked. It was easy. It didn't take them long to install a hitch and hook it up. It was light and futuristic. I didn't suppose Dennis Hopper would mind that little added fillip of contemporary technology. If Jake hadn't found it too decadent, perhaps it wasn't. I drove it home; Steph and I packed our stuff in its luggage space.

Early next morning, we dressed for the road. As I put on the Cotta sweatshirt Rotz had given me, I wondered if, in 30 or 40 years, I might be trapped in some assisted living complex and would notice some clueless kid in his 50s or 60s, wandering around bumping into things. And maybe he'd even search me out, and I'd tell him about Rotz and the stories. But for the time being, I locked up the house and made sure the alarm system was set.

Steph and I donned helmets, boots, and gloves and rode away, just like that, heading west. We would ride for as long as we wanted, eating and sleeping where we pleased. No schedules. Only whim travel. There were hotels and motels and restaurants whenever we needed them. There would be campfires in isolated expanses of deserts and forests. We had money to burn. There was nothing to it.

I took the freeway out of town. In no time we were in the Dakotas. The engine roared between our legs. The rising sun filled my mirrors and warmed us. We were free at last. It was, well, like a ballet…

Fuck the world. I was finally out of its grasp, at least for a little while. I didn't give a damn what it tried to do to me. We are *Men of Cotta*, I said to myself as the Harley screamed along the highway, cruising at high speed, the wind whipping my hair and the fringe of Rotz's leather jacket. We don't take shit from anybody. You fuck with us, you pay the price.

I opened up the helmet mike to Steph. Together, we found a starting note we could agree on – *we, we, we, weee…* Then we sang at the top of our lungs…

We're a buncha bastards
Scum of the earth…

July, 2011
Tait Lake